The Stranger said,

"If that's a weapon you're reaching for, don't."

But Otto didn't listen. He reached. The stranger broke an empty wine bottle and slashed Otto's hand. Otto screamed and stopped reaching.

The stranger said, "Talk."

Otto talked. When he had heard what he wanted to hear, the stranger said, "Tell A.K. I'm coming, and don't forget the name. It's Carter, Nick Carter."

NICK CARTER IS IT!

FROM THE NICK CARTER
KILLMASTER SERIES

KILLING GAMES

KILL MASTER

NICK CARTER

JOVE BOOKS, NEW YORK

KILLING GAMES

A Jove book / published by arrangement with
The Condé Nast Publications, Inc.

PRINTING HISTORY
Jove edition / August 1987

ISBN: 0-515-09112-X

Jove Books are published by The Berkley Publishing Group,
200 Madison Avenue, New York, New York 10016.
The name "JOVE" and the "J" logo
are trademarks belonging to Jove Publications, Inc.

PRINTED IN THE UNITED STATES OF AMERICA

10 9 8 7 6 5 4 3 2 1

Dedicated to the men of the
Secret Services of the
United States of America

ONE

SIX YEARS AGO

The sky was gray and the air crisp with a strong breeze blowing inland over the wild Welsh coastline.

Anthony Hobbs-Nelson applied the Land-Rover's brakes and pulled a West Country map from the glove compartment. When it was spread out over the steering wheel, he traced the route they had taken with a finger.

"You are lost."

The way she said it, with her heavy French accent, it came out, "Ou aire loosed." It brought a smile to his face, the first since they had left the inn at Port Eynon early that morning.

"I am not loosed," he replied. "Right there, Worm's Head."

She smiled herself, leaned across the seat, and kissed him. "I love you, dear Tony."

"And I love you, Nanette."

"Then drive hurry to this Worm's Head before your wife is starved!"

The Land-Rover surged forward, and minutes later they were on a bluff overlooking the Bristol Channel six hundred feet below.

"Oh, Tony, Tony, be careful, *mon amour!* Is dangerous!"

"As a secret agent," he growled, a ferocious scowl on his face, "I must live dangerously. Let's eat."

He set the hand brake and grabbed a picnic hamper and blankets from the rear seat.

"I will do it," she said.

"I'll help."

Together, they spread the blankets and unpacked wine and food from the hamper.

As they ate, he fell back into the state of moody silence. It had been his constant companion for the last two weeks, since giving his resignation to his British intelligence superiors at MI6.

"You will still go to the United States, Tony?" she asked softly, sensing his mood.

He nodded. "I must."

"This game of yours, it is so important?"

"It could be. The old school boys here don't think so, but I might be able to convince the Americans."

The hard set of his jaw and the now-familiar glassy quality that crept into his eyes made her look away.

She knew very little about her husband's work, only what he would—or could—tell her. Most of what he did for British intelligence was carried out in what he called the "think tank."

"We play games," he had said. "War games, economic games, nuclear games. Just dream up games."

Now he had come up with a game that had scared him to death, and his superiors had called it preposterous, useless, and unfeasible. That was why Anthony Hobbs-Nelson had resigned and vowed to take his game to Washington and the American CIA.

The distant but swiftly approaching roar of a motorcycle broke into their reverie.

"Sounds like we have company," he said.

He rose and climbed to the top of a low hill. About half a mile away, a lone rider on a powerful machine was moving directly toward him. The motorcyclist was coming full tilt, raising a dust devil behind him.

Dammit, Hobbs-Nelson thought. *We come all the way out here to be alone, and this idiot picks the same place to play with his noisy toy.*

The black-clad rider swiveled to a halt in front of him, killed the engine, and leaned the machine over on its kickstand. He dismounted and shoved up the dark visor on his helmet.

"Well, I'll be damned. What the hell are you doing in the wilds of Wales?" Hobbs-Nelson exclaimed.

"Hello, Tony. Where's your lovely bride?"

"Back there by the Rover. Did you follow us out from London . . ."

But the rider had walked past him and started down the hill.

"Look, old chap, I don't know what you want, but Nanette and I . . ."

She looked up and smiled at the black-clad figure. "Oh, hello! What—"

Nanette got only a brief glimpse of the oddly shaped gun before the dart struck her in the neck.

Hobbs-Nelson didn't see the gun at all, but he saw his wife fall to the ground. He cried out in alarm and anger, and lunged for the cyclist.

He had one hand on the man's shoulder, spinning him around, when the air-powered dart gun was pressed against his own chest.

"You bastards! You—"

It was all Anthony Hobbs-Nelson got out before the powerful tranquilizer rendered his limbs, then his body, then his mind, useless.

The rider was a model of efficiency. He gathered up the blankets and the picnic hamper and placed them in the Land-Rover. Then Anthony and Nanette Hobbs-Nelson were placed in the front seats and secured with safety belts. Carefully, the sliverlike darts were removed from their necks. When this was done, he started the engine and engaged the gears.

It was a little tricky maneuvering the unconscious man's leg and foot to press the accelerator and race the engine, but he managed.

He waited only long enough to see the Land-Rover crash into the sea and slip from sight in the murky waters of the Bristol Channel before jumping back on his machine and roaring away.

TWO

NOW

Cory Howard stretched his six-foot-five frame in the rear of the big car and peered through the open window. The only light was from kerosene lanterns behind burlap curtains in the row of mountaintop village shacks.

Far below and ten miles in the distance, the lights of Uruguay's capital, Montevideo, cast a hazy blue-white arc in the sky.

"Do you really think he'll come?"

The speaker was Lilly Kalensky. She was a pretty woman with a small, boyish, delicate yet muscular body. Her nose was straight and fine, her cheekbones high, and her eyes brightly blue and watchful.

Fifteen years earlier she had walked a month by night to escape Hungary. Most of the way she had carried her baby sister on her back and dragged her mother. Along the way she had stolen food and killed three Communist border guards to survive and escape.

Then on a frigid January night they had rendezvoused with Cory Howard and he had spirited them across Yugoslavia and eventually to freedom.

Howard had been with MI6 then. Before that, he had been in the elite British SAS.

Eventually he had grown weary of the frustrating bureaucracy of the services, and resigned.

That was when he started Salvation Limited, and Lilly Kalensky was only one of many people he had hired and trained to work for him. He counseled international corporations, teaching their executives how to combat terrorism and elude kidnappings. Often those same executives didn't heed his warnings or install his recommended safeguards.

When it happened that one of their key people was kidnapped, Salvation Limited was brought in to negotiate the ransom or rescue the victim.

On this night, the victim was Marcel Longchamp, the top geologist for the French corporation specializing in valuable industrial metals.

He had been snatched two weeks earlier from the streets of Rosario in Argentina, just across the border from Uruguay. The company had sent out the word to the Hunter— as Cory Howard was now called.

The kidnappers referred to themselves as "freedom fighters." In actual fact, they were nothing but a bunch of mountain *banditos* out for a quick buck.

They were asking five million ransom for Longchamp. His company didn't want to pay five. They didn't even want to pay one. They offered the Hunter $250,000 to bring their boy out.

"Did you hear me?" she asked again.

"What?" Howard said, lighting the cigarette that had been dangling from his lips for the last five minutes.

"I think he got cold feet," Lilly said. "I don't think he's coming."

"He'll come. He's a born little rat. He'd rather take the cash offer I made and inform on his pals than take a chance that something screws up and Longchamp is killed. Then he'd have to run for the rest of his life. He'll come."

The last word was barely uttered when they both saw a flash of movement on one of the hillsides above the shacks. Minutes later, a man in faded blue jeans, a loose cotton shirt, and a battered hat pulled low over his eyes trotted up to the car's open window.

"Hello, Pepe."

"You got the money, señor?"

"I've got the money, Pepe," Howard replied, holding up a fat manilla envelope. "You got the place?"

"*Sí.* They are holding him in an old mining camp in the hills above Salto. I drew a map and sketched the layout of the buildings for you."

"Give it to me."

The man shook his head. "The money, señor. I will have to travel a very long distance if my *compadres* find out what I have done."

Lilly Kalensky sat quietly in the front seat, her hands on the wheel. Her eyes lifted, focusing on Howard's image in the rearview mirror.

Howard opened the envelope in his hand and fanned the bills. Leaving several of them showing, he laid the envelope on the seat beside him. "The sketches."

Saliva practically dripped from Pepe's lips as his eyes gazed steadily at the money. Then his hand slid into his shirt and he handed Howard two folded sheets of paper. At the same time, Howard's eyes flicked once forward and he nodded his head slightly.

"Take your money, Pepe."

Eagerly, the informant reached through the window. His hand was on the envelope and the money when the electric window slid upward. The window caught him beneath the armpit.

In a sudden, trapped frenzy, he began to squirm, working his body furiously in an attempt to pull himself free.

Lilly Kalensky had already turned in the driver's seat. Carefully, she aligned the silenced Walther PPK in both hands.

She shot Pepe twice, once in the right eye and once in the center of the forehead.

Howard immediately buzzed the window down, allowing the body to fall to the dusty road.

Lilly dropped the Walther to the seat beside her and started the car. As she sped away, she opened the other three windows to let the smell of cordite disperse.

"Where to?"

"Back to Montevideo," Howard said. "We'll need a helicopter."

He was already going over the two sheets of paper.

"How many in the mining camp?" she asked.

"Four, according to Pepe." ·

Lilly smiled. "A piece of cake, as the Americans say."

It was the silent hour before dawn when Cory Howard crawled over the last jutting rocks and looked down at the camp.

There was a large central house, four small shacks, and two vehicles—an ancient truck and an old Chevrolet. A small stream wound its way through the area, with a small bridge over it leading to the house.

There was only one light. It came from the corner room of the house.

Carefully, silently, Howard eased himself off the ledge and onto the roof. From there it was a short drop to a clearing at the rear of the house.

Nothing moved anywhere. The old, unpainted building slumped dejectedly, as if thinking about someday collapsing completely. It was roofed with split wooden shakes and sat on round foundation blocks cut from raw logs. A section of rusting stovepipe extended above the roof at the rear and was guyed with baling wire.

Howard crept the full length of the rear. There was no door in back.

That was good. The front was the only exit, unless they dived out one or more of the three rear windows.

There was no sign of an outside lookout or a dog.

They were awfully dumb, Howard thought, or awfully sure of themselves.

He slipped noiselessly up to the lighted window and peered inside. There were three of them, two asleep on the floor and one in an alcoholic or drug haze with a pair of earphones on his head.

Howard moved to the darkened window at the opposite rear corner. The inside door to the hall was open. In the dimness he saw two figures. One was lying flat out on a mattress in one corner. The other was sitting with his back against the wall, snoring loudly.

Okay, Howard thought, *which is which?*

But at least he knew the room. Also, the stovepipe on the roof led down to an old-fashioned pot-bellied wood burner squatting in the center of the room.

Howard retraced his steps to the center of the house and slipped a backpack from his shoulders. From it he took two long strings of flash grenades.

One string he left intact, and he fastened it all around the lighted window. The other string he separated into six individual grenades. Four of these he hung on his belt. The remaining two were attached to a long pull wire.

Then he climbed back up onto the roof. Gently, he lowered the grenades down the stovepipe until they hit bottom in the belly of the old stove.

He took a penlight flash from his pocket and pointed it toward a strand of trees thirty yards in front of the house. Two quick flashes brought an answering reply from the trees.

Playing the wire out, he climbed down to the ground. The trip wire from the window string he held in his teeth. The silenced Walther he held in his left hand; his right grasped the trip wire to the grenades in the stove.

It would all be a matter of timing.

Using his wrist, he pushed a pair of smoked-glass goggles from his forehead down over his eyes. He took a deep breath, let it out slowly, and pulled the trip wire in his right hand.

The blast and the glare were somewhat subdued in the belly of the stove, but the explosion was still enough to raise hell in the room and illuminate the two occupants.

The one who had been sitting against the wall lurched to his feet, clawing a big magnum from his belt.

Howard put two slugs right through the glass into the center of his chest, and pulled the second trip wire.

Next door, night turned into day, and shattered glass went everywhere.

Howard used the long silencer to break out the rest of the window, and dived through. Outside the door, he could already hear chaotic shouting and footsteps pounding down the hall.

He pulled the pin on two of the grenades, threw them into the hall, and slammed the door.

He turned to the man crouched on the mattress. "Monsieur Marcel Longchamp?"

"*Oui*, but what—"

"Don't talk, do! Hurry—the window!"

The man's hands were cuffed in front of his body. Howard had him separate his wrists until the chain was on the sill, then he severed it with a slug from the Walther.

"Out, fast!"

With a little help from Howard, the man went out the window with the Hunter practically on his back.

Pulling Longchamp behind him, they scooted around the side of the house, ran to the stream, and dropped behind the protection of its bank.

The flash grenades had started two fires, one in the hallway and another in the room that had held the three men.

As Howard watched, one man dived out the window that he and Longchamp had just used. He had a shotgun and was waving it around wildly, looking for something to shoot at. Finally he ran around to the front, shouting.

The other two bolted from the front door just as Howard lobbed the two remaining grenades toward the front of the house.

The shotgun waver got off one barrel, but Howard was already back down in the safety of the stream bed.

The grenades went off, lighting up the trio like ducks in a shooting gallery. Lilly Kalensky stepped from the trees with the Uzi in her hands blazing. The Walther was jumping in Howard's hands, leaving the three men in the center of the deadly crossfire.

It was over in seconds.

"That's it, Lilly," Howard growled, rising and walking quickly to the carnage, dragging Longchamp with him.

"Oh, my God," Longchamp cried, staring down at the bloody bodies, "what have you done?"

"Killed them. C'mon, let's get the hell out of here."

It was noon in Paris, and hot. Outside the twelve-story building just off the Rue Saint-Honoré that housed the home offices of StarFire Mining and Industrial Research, heat waves rose like undulating belly dancers to the penthouse office suite of the company president.

Denis Jeansoulin sat behind his massive desk, staring at the center telephone of three near his right hand. He had discarded his jacket hours earlier, but it hadn't stemmed the flow of perspiration from his pores. His white-on-white shirt was soaked through and moisture from his face dripped steadily from his chin.

It was a cold sweat brought on by the reality that his life and the life of the company that his grandfather had founded more than a century before depended on a single telephone call.

When the center phone rang, Jeansoulin nearly fell from his chair as he grabbed the receiver. "Yes, yes?"

"This is Howard. He's out and unharmed."

"Thank God," Jeansoulin sighed with relief. "Where are you?"

"On Lake Salado, about five miles outside Buenos Aires. I requisitioned someone's summer house. Where do you want him delivered?"

"Wait two hours and then drive him into Buenos Aires, to the airport. I'll have our company plane standing by."

"And the other half of my money?"

"I'll notify our Zurich bank. It will be in your account within the hour."

"Nice doing business with you, Monsieur Jeansoulin."

"You are a savior, Monsieur Howard."

Denis Jeansoulin hung up and eased back in his chair for a moment of sublime relief before calling his man in Buenos Aires to prepare the plane.

It was over. In a few hours, Marcel Longchamp would be in Paris. The information in his head would be more than enough proof to the bankers holding the gigantic Star-Fire loans that the company was now solvent.

Platinum—thousands of ounces of raw platinum—and

its sister element, palladium, in easily minable deposits.

StarFire's South American leases would be worth billions.

Denis Jeansoulin mopped his face and reached for the phone.

In the receptionist's office, Jeansoulin's private secretary, Henri Liard, waited until his boss had hung up before he replaced the receiver of his own phone.

Liard left his office and took an elevator to the ground floor. Near a newspaper and magazine kiosk he slipped into a phone booth. Quickly, he dialed a long series of numbers that would connect him to a voice in London.

Liard didn't know the owner of the voice: he had never met either the man or the woman who always answered. But the StarFire executive secretary knew that both of them—or their control—were wealthy and powerful... powerful enough to engineer a takeover of a huge mining conglomerate like StarFire. And, if his research was correct, StarFire would not be the first nor the last industrial mining and ore refining company that had fallen to their sword.

And when that takeover happened, Henri Liard would be much more than an executive assistant or glorified secretary.

The London phone was picked up on the third ring. "Yes?"

"This is Liard in Paris."

He could hear the switchover being made: clicks, buzzes, then another ring. It was a dummy phone-through operation handled by computers punched up by some faceless person in some small drab office who only knew codes and names. StarFire itself used such numbers for its clandestine industrial espionage.

"One moment."

It was a full minute, during which Liard studied the constant flow of beautiful Parisian women coming and going outside the booth.

Soon, very soon, he thought, he could pick and choose.

"Bonjour, mon ami. What do you have for us?" It was the woman this time instead of the gravel-voiced man. *Mon Dieu,* Liard mused, she had the voice of a three-thousand-franc whore.

"Longchamp. The Hunter got him out."

There were several seconds of silence from the other end. Liard fidgeted, but he knew better than to speak. The woman was thinking, weighing alternatives.

"That is too bad, Henri," the sultry feminine voice finally said. "It was a major stroke of luck, a grand coincidence, when these Latinos kidnapped him. It saved us the trouble of intercepting him ourselves."

"The Hunter has Longchamp in Buenos Aires. He's taking him to the airport in two hours. He will be in Paris long before the meeting tomorrow."

"I see. Where in Buenos Aires?"

"A cottage on a lake outside the city, Lake Salado. I have no name. Howard said it was a summer cottage, empty. He 'requisitioned' it."

"It should be easy to find. You have done well, Henri."

"Merci, madame."

"Our mutual benefactor will see that you are rewarded handsomely, I am sure."

"Merci beaucoup."

"Au revoir, mon ami."

Henri Liard couldn't suppress the ripple of fear and revulsion that ran through his body as he took the elevator back to the twelfth floor.

He didn't want to consider what was going to happen to Marcel Longchamp.

But down deep he knew, and it scared the hell out of him.

He thought of the woman. Sometimes, at night in a dream, the woman's voice came to him. He wondered if she had the body to match the voice.

He wondered if he would ever meet her.

Then he again thought of Longchamp, and decided he didn't want to meet the woman.

Lilly Kalensky saw the speedboat first and called to Cory Howard. He joined her and peered out through the crack in the closed drapes.

A man, dark, with a mustache and wearing a white shirt and shorts, climbed up to the pier from the boat. He turned and held his hand out to an attractive, long-limbed woman in a bathing suit and short terry-cloth robe. When the woman was on the pier, they both reached back into the boat and came up with suitcases.

"The owners?" Lilly asked anxiously.

"Could be," Howard replied. "Christ, nobody comes out to the lakes around here for at least another two weeks."

"Can we bluff them?"

"We'll have to try. Put the Uzi in the case. We don't want to spook them. I'll give them some kind of a story. Wake up Longchamp and get him ready to roll."

Lilly nodded and moved back into the bowels of the house. Howard slipped the Walther under his belt at the small of his back and pulled on a jacket. He then plastered on his most engaging smile and walked out the front door.

"Hello there, you must be the owners. Had an accident with my own boat last night . . ."

They stood, staring, the man seeming perplexed. But the woman seemed only nervous. Her eyes kept darting over Howard's shoulder.

The bags were expensive, Howard noted, and the woman's jewelry indicated wealth. They were definitely Latin, but still . . .

Suddenly, from behind him inside the house, came the unmistakable chatter of machine gun fire. Howard whirled, working on instinct, grabbing at the Walther in his belt.

The huge windows on either side of the door burst outward and slugs stitched holes through the door itself.

Howard's attention was drawn to the house for only a second, but it was long enough. The suitcase in the man's hand cracked across Howard's elbow just as his arm was going up. The Walther flew from his hand, clattered over the wooden pier, and fell into the water.

The woman already had a small-caliber pistol out and was firing wildly as the man swung again with the suitcase.

Howard rolled to the side. The suitcase missed, but he felt one of the slugs burn a path along his left side. He managed to grab the man by the front of his shirt. At the same time, he lunged with his shoulder and drove the man into the woman's still-spurting revolver.

The man screamed and his eyes went wild with shock as he slipped to the deck of the pier.

The revolver clicked on empty. Before Howard could reach the woman, she threw the empty gun at him and dived into the water. In seconds she was lost beneath the pier.

He started toward the house, when suddenly the door burst open and Lilly was backing toward him, the Uzi in her hands spraying the doorway and window.

"Cory, Cory, where are you!"

"Right behind you!" he cried. "Longchamp?"

"Dead. There are at least six of them!"

"The boat!" Howard yelled. "Keep coming!"

He dived into the boat. The keys were in the ignition.

By the time the engine roared to life, answering fire had started coming from the house.

Lilly was on her belly on the pier, the Uzi blazing.

"Lilly, roll . . . roll into the boat!"

She rolled, and the instant he saw her secure in the well, Howard jammed the throttle to full. The bow lifted and the powerful inboard sailed into the lake. Out of the corner of his eye he could see spurts in the water and hear the thuds as a few rounds found the boat.

He was practically sitting down, driving by looking up at the tops of the trees. The windshield above him shattered, and suddenly the firing stopped.

He chanced a look. They were thirty yards short of the opposite side of the lake. Directly in front of them was a short stretch of sand backed with heavy undergrowth.

"Hang on!" he shouted, and steered directly for it.

The bow crunched, and then he could hear the underside of the boat scrape over the low foliage. They came to rest at a tilt and Howard cut the engine.

"Come on!"

"Cory . . ."

He turned. He knew she was hit by the low gurgle in her voice. She lay on her back in the well of the boat, a dark stain spreading across the front of her black sweater.

Gently, Howard pulled the sweater up to the bottom of her breasts.

"Oh, Jesus . . ."

"Bad?" Her eyes opened, staring glassily up, through him, at the sky.

"Yes, Lilly . . . bad."

"Wouldn't you know it?" she said, and coughed. "He was dead, Cory. They came through the rear windows firing. They got him right away. My God, they cut him in half!"

"Take it easy, Lilly."

"No, Cory, listen to me . . . this is important. I know one of them. That night . . . when you brought us out . . . in Subotica . . ."

"Lilly . . ."

"No, listen! That man who met us, the one with the low husky voice, the one who could hardly speak . . ."

"In Yugoslavia?" Howard was trying to concentrate, to drag his mind back fifteen years.

"You said he had been stabbed once in the throat . . . that was why his voice was like that."

"Oh, my God, Longbone . . . Wolf Longbone?"

"Yes, Wolf, yes . . . Cory, my sis—"

"Lilly . . ."

Her head rolled to the side and a steady river of blood curled from the corner of her mouth.

Denis Jeansoulin hummed as he poured champagne into a crystal glass.

It was over. He had won. The banks would be pacified, the stockholders would back off, and the overseas vultures, whoever they were, would go in search of another company to rape.

When the telephone rang he answered it with a jaunty air, not noticing it was the special line he had set up since the first night of the kidnapping.

"Hello?"

"Jeansoulin, you son of a bitch!"

"What? Who is this?"

"This is Howard, and don't tell me you can't recognize my voice by now, you bloody bastard. What the hell are you trying to pull?"

Suddenly the sweat started again and the hair at the back of his neck started to itch. "What is it? What is the matter?"

"The matter is, damn you, if you wanted Longchamp dead, why bring him out? Why not let the kidnappers do it? Or were you afraid they wouldn't go through with their threat?"

"*Mon Dieu,* Monsieur Howard, what are you saying?"

"I'm saying we were hit!"

"Hit? I don't understand. Hit?"

"Longchamp is dead! Who did you tip off or tell where we were?"

"No one! I swear it, no one!" Jeansoulin choked.

"Well, somebody found out," Howard hissed. "They used two decoys. I thought . . ."

The voice continued, but Denis Jeansoulin heard no more. By instinct he hung up the phone as his body slumped back in the chair.

It wasn't over.

Yes, it was. For him.

In a trance, he opened the center drawer of his desk. The champagne glass was jiggled from his hand as he reached and found the .45 Colt that his father had carried in the liberation of Paris.

His mind was a total blank when he put the barrel in his mouth and pressed the trigger with both thumbs.

THREE

Other than two blue-haired elderly ladies, a pair of pin-striped business types, and Nick Carter, the first class section of the big Boeing was empty.

The two ladies were chattering about how homesick they were going to be, gone from the States for two whole weeks touring the English countryside. Between ranting about inept politicians and the lack of moral fiber in the American youth of today, the two men tried to convince the two attractive hostesses to shack up with them the first night in London.

Carter was thinking about the odd aspects of the last twenty-four hours that had put him on this London flight.

The original request had come from a CIA deputy, John Hutchins. He had asked the chief of AXE operations for a night meet in the wilds of Virginia on a matter of "utmost priority."

Since Cory Howard's name had been mentioned, David Hawk had included Carter on the meet. The AXE Killmaster had run two missions in the old days with Howard, and since the man's retirement from MI6 they had worked the rescue of a kidnapped American scientist from Iran.

Hutchins, a rather prissy little man with eyes set too close together and a nervous habit of cracking his knuckles, had come right to the point.

"MI6 thinks they have a rogue agent."

"Cory Howard?" Carter said, not trying to hide the surprise in his voice. "He's free-lance, has his own company. It's been years since he left the service. How can he be a rogue?" Hutchins smiled, showing too many teeth above a depressed chin. "Mr. Carter, I'm sure you, of all people, know that once you're in you're always in ... even after retirement."

Carter tensed at the little man's condescending tone. He thought for a second of reaching with thumb and forefinger and ripping the little bastard's button nose from his pudgy face.

A look at Hawk's scowl made him sit back. As usual, the head of AXE was sitting calmly, preferring to disregard the froth until he had heard the meat.

"Other than being brought in as a free-lance for us a time or two in the past," Hawk said, "why talk to us about Howard?"

"The request comes from Sir Phillip Avery," Hutchins replied. "I work quite closely with Sir Phillip as liaison between CIA and MI6. Two days ago, Sir Charles Martin got an extortion demand from Cory Howard for five million pounds."

"Bullshit," Carter growled.

"I'm afraid not."

"Do you have a copy of the letter?" Hawk asked.

"No, but the gist of it is that if Mr. Howard does not get his five million, he has threatened to, as he puts it, 'blow the lid on Sir Charles and both services.'"

Hawk leaned forward, the cigar in his clenched teeth creating a wreath of smoke around his head. "I can understand why they are requesting us to aid in the investigation if we're part of the extortion demand, but where does Sir Charles Martin come in?"

Hutchins leaned forward. "I must have the word of both of you that what I am about to reveal concerning Sir Charles must never leave this room."

Both Hawk and Carter shrugged, signifying that such a request from men on their level was superfluous, even insulting, but they nodded their agreement.

"I assume," Hutchins continued, "that you know a little of Sir Charles Martin's background. He inherited vast wealth in his youth, and became somewhat of an economic *wunderkind*. He multiplied his inheritance a thousand times over, acquiring companies all over the world."

"And," Hawk growled, "he has intelligence connections."

"Exactly. For years, literally since he began his remarkable rise, he has devoted a large portion of his resources to intelligence gathering for MI6 and MI5. This has been done on a completely secret basis to allow Sir Charles a great deal of latitude. Eventually, of course, we also took advantage of Sir Charles's patriotism. Only a few select people know of Sir Charles's involvement with our intelligence agencies."

"Who?" Hawk asked pointedly.

Hutchins sniffed. "I am not at liberty to divulge that information."

Through the smoke of his own cigarette Carter saw a tiny muscle jump in Hawk's cheek. The man's jaw clamped so hard it was amazing the cigar stayed together.

Carter knew what was going on in the old man's mind. For years, David Hawk had been the chief of supersecret, superpowerful AXE. As such, he was one of the "very select" people in American intelligence. If he wasn't privy to Sir Charles Martin's role, who the hell was?

"I see," Hawk said, doing a marvelous job of keeping a lid on his anger. "Just what is it you want with us?"

"It has been agreed that an agent of MI6 *and* one of ours

interview Sir Charles and try to get to the bottom of all this." Hutchins turned to Carter. "How soon can you leave for England?"

"As soon as I decide to send him," Hawk snapped.

Carter smiled.

Hutchins fidgeted. "Of course. I'm sorry, Mr. Hawk, I didn't mean to overstep my authority. I just want to stress Sir Charles's immense worth over the years, and the help he can give us in the future. We would hate to lose that alliance. You see, we owe Sir Charles."

"Okay," Hawk sighed, "we haven't anything immediately pressing right now."

Hutchins stood. "There is one more thing . . ."

"Which is?" Carter asked.

"We would like to keep this as quiet as possible until we know more about it. We would appreciate it if you did not contact any of your people, or ours, in England. Needless to say, that goes for MI6 and MI5 staff as well."

"Who is the MI6 half of the interview?" Carter asked.

"Her name is Sharon Purdue. She is a close associate of Sir Phillip Avery, and has some knowledge of Sir Charles's involvement. Also, like you, Mr. Carter, Miss Purdue has been close to Cory Howard."

"How close?"

Hutchins flushed. "Uh, bedroom close, to put it in the vernacular. Mr. Howard was, for quite some time, Miss Purdue's lover. Here is a private number in London where she can be reached."

Carter pocketed the sheet of paper without looking at it.

The handshaking good-byes were slightly strained. Carter and Hawk wasted no time getting out of the Virginia farmhouse and to their car.

Neil Griffin and Gig Clark, Hawk's two bodyguards who would look more comfortable in Green Bay Packer uniforms than three-piece suits, were waiting.

"Where to?" Griffin asked after closing the rear door behind his boss and climbing into the driver's seat.

"The office," Hawk said, and lit a fresh cigar.

"The office" was the building housing Amalgamated Press and Wire Services on Dupont Circle. A few rooms actually functioned as a wire service, but the rest was all AXE.

"Well?" Hawk asked at last, when they had gained the interstate back toward Washington.

Carter shrugged. "I think I know Cory Howard, and it doesn't sound right. He was a little sour when he left the service and started his own business, sure, but this doesn't fit."

Hawk nodded. "But, as I remember, his fees are pretty high and he does live well."

"Granted, but why a shakedown on this Sir Charles Martin specifically?"

"Let's hope you find out in London."

"I'd like a complete dossier on Sir Charles, and also an update on Howard."

"It will be waiting for you tomorrow"—Hawk paused, checking his watch—"tonight, at the airport."

They were just pulling into the underground garage at Amalgamated when Carter voiced the bottom-line thought that had been on both their minds.

"If Sir Charles Martin was feeding us so much good information, wouldn't John Starkey, Burt Esterman, or Jonathan Hart-Davis in London be one of the select people who knew about him?"

"Don't know," Hawk said, "but I mean to find out."

John Starkey was AXE liaison to the Oval Office. As such, he was privy to all CIA intelligence passing across the President's desk.

Burt Esterman was the link between CIA and AXE, and was privy to everything Starkey saw.

Carter knew that, first thing in the morning, those two men would be summoned to Hawk's office.

"Should I see Hart-Davis in London?" Carter asked.

"No, not until we know more. If Sir Charles really has been that valuable, we had better respect Hutchins's request for secrecy."

The two men parted in the garage. Hawk headed for his private elevator, his two shadows in tow. The Killmaster knew that the old man would probably be up the rest of the night, digging.

Carter got in his own car and headed across town to his Georgetown digs.

Stripped save a bathrobe and a tall scotch, he opened his safe and dug out his own file on Cory Howard. He thought he remembered a connection.

He had, but it took him a good half hour to find it.

Lilly Kalensky had worked for Howard. Carter had never met her, but the Killmaster had surmised that the relationship had gone a little deeper than just employer and employee.

About a year and a half ago, he had gotten a call from Lilly Kalensky, using Howard as a reference. She had wanted Carter to give her sister a hand in locating an apartment and settling into the States. The girl was going to be a freshman at Georgetown University.

Carter had done just that, but he couldn't recall the girl's name or the exact address of her apartment.

Then he found it: Jova Kalen. Now he remembered that she had dropped the last three letters, thinking it made the name sound more "American."

He checked the telephone directory, found the address was still the same, and jotted down the telephone number.

With the clock set for seven, he stretched out and was immediately asleep.

At one minute before that hour, his own mental clock awakened him.

Fumbling, he found the phone and the slip of paper he had placed near it before crashing.

A pleasant, self-assured voice with only the slightest trace of an accent answered on the third ring. "Hello?"

"Could I speak to Jova Kalen, please."

"This is she."

Carter thought he detected an odd note of alarm in the girl's voice. "Jova, I don't know if you remember me or not, Nick Carter?"

"Oh, of course, Mr. Carter! How could I ever forget the help you gave me?"

"I know you probably have classes all day, but I wonder if you'd have time for lunch?"

"With you, of course. When and where?"

"How about Pallon's? It's close to your apartment. You name the time."

"I finish my last class of the day at one-thirty. How about two? Is that too late?"

"Two would be fine. See you then."

He hung up and rolled over to grab a couple more hours' sleep, thinking that her voice had sounded very relieved when he had told her his name.

It was eleven when he started into the kitchen and made coffee. By twelve he had showered, shaved, and dressed. A small flight bag took all the essentials for a short trip. If it became a long one, he would, as usual, buy new along the way and discard the old.

AXE business was very hard on clothing and personal items in the field.

In the false bottom of his flight bag he stored the major equipment of his trade: a 9mm Luger he affectionately called Wilhelmina, and a pencil-thin stiletto, dubbed Hugo, in a spring-activated chamois sheath.

The last thing he did before leaving was fish once again through Howard's file until he came up with two solid examples of the man's signature and handwriting.

Leaving his car garaged, he cabbed to Pallon's, arriving fifteen minutes early, and checked his bag with the cloakroom attendant.

"I'll be expecting a young lady. My name is Carter," he announced to the maître d'.

"Of course, sir, this way."

Carter ordered three fingers of Chivas over a single ice cube and, by habit, checked out everyone around him as he waited. It was the normal crowd . . . young, rising attorneys, a few politicians, and the ladies who lunch.

At precisely two, the maître d' approached the table with Jova Kalen in tow.

She wouldn't have made Miss Cheerleader, but if she stopped fighting it, she would have been a pretty girl, Carter thought. She was above average height, with a slender, curvaceous figure that she tried to hide under a formless sweater and a skirt that had twelve-too-many yards of material. Her dark hair was cut short and combed back from a broad forehead. Her eyebrows were full, and the long black lashes that swept up from the dark, no-nonsense eyes were her own.

Carter kissed her lightly on the cheek. "I'm glad you remembered me."

"How could I forget you?" she said and smiled. "You were my first crush in America!"

The talk, through a glass of wine and salad, was superficial chitchat, mostly of school, how she was fitting in, the fact that she loved the States and never wanted to leave.

Carter detected the same strain he had sensed on the

phone, but talked around it until dessert and coffee.

"Jova, I have to admit that I have an ulterior motive for this lunch," he said at last.

Her body tensed slightly. "Yes?"

"Your sister, Lilly. I'd like to get in touch with her."

Her lower lip curled between her teeth. Then a heavy sigh. Then she leaned forward and it poured out.

"So would I. Since I have been here, we talk at least twice a week. Either Lilly calls me or I call her. But I haven't heard from her in a month, and I'm worried. Also, she sends me a check the first of every month, never misses. This month it didn't come."

"Do you need money?"

"Oh, no, I never spend all that she sends anyway. It's just not like Lilly to miss the check."

"Jova, I want to ask you something."

"Yes?"

"Do you remember Cory Howard?"

A slight flush crept into her face. "Of course. Like you, he did so much for us. And he's very close to my sister."

"How close?"

Now it was a deep blush. "The last time I visited Lilly, they slept together. She told me it was nothing serious, they were only part-time lovers."

"Did you know that your sister worked for Cory Howard?"

"No," she replied, and then that broad forehead furrowed. "In fact, I really don't know what Lilly does for money. Oh, dear, is it illegal?"

"No, not at all," Carter replied, and quickly went on. "Tell me about the last time you talked to Lilly."

Jova closed her eyes, concentrated, and spoke. "Yes, she said she was leaving the islands for a few days on business, and she would call me the moment she got back."

"The islands?"

"The Cayman Islands. She has a villa on Cayman Brac."

"Is there any other place to reach her?"

"Yes, a flat in London . . . Mayfair. Nick, is something wrong? Has something happened to Lilly?"

"I don't think so."

"Then why are you asking about her?"

"Actually, Jova, I would like to find Cory Howard."

She shrugged. "He has a house in England . . . Cornwall, I think. That's all I know."

Carter could see in her eyes that she wanted to know more, not accepting the little bit he had told her. He moved the conversation away from Howard and her sister until they hit the street.

"I promise you, Jova, if I see or hear anything about Lilly, I'll be in touch."

"Thank you," she said. "Oh, there's one other person that might be of help, Rita Lyon. She runs a cocktail lounge in George Town. Lilly and Rita were very close friends. She might know something."

"Have you contacted her?"

"No, but I was about to."

"Don't," Carter said. "I'll do it for you."

He walked her to her apartment and grabbed a cab to Dulles.

It was a pretty good chance, he mused as he boarded the plane, that if Lilly Kalensky had gone underground, so had Cory Howard.

But why?

Heathrow never changed; even at that early hour it was a beehive of activity. Carter took the moving walkway, then went down the escalators to the baggage claim. Somewhere in the mass of humanity around him he knew there would be MI6 people checking every face.

Utmost secrecy, Hutchins had said. *Don't contact any of theirs, or ours.*

If any of the MI6 or MI5 people at Heathrow were old hands, it would be less than an hour before Carter's presence in London would be known and wondered about.

Screw Hutchins.

Carter collected his bag and found a phone booth. He dialed the number from memory.

"Yes?"

"Sharon Purdue?"

"Yes."

"Carter. I'm at Heathrow."

"My flat is in Cherries Street, just off Tottenham Court Road. The number is twelve."

"An hour," Carter said, and hung up.

As the cab sailed into London, past the vastness of Victoria Station, Park Lane, and then the Marble Arch, Carter couldn't help but feel that if this whole thing were for real, then Cory Howard had really slipped a cog.

And if a man as dangerous as Howard *had* gone off the deep end, it was going to be one hell of a job to nail him.

"Here ya are, guv, number twelve."

Carter paid the driver and mounted the stoop of a recently renovated town house. He punched the buzzer marked S. PURDUE, and, when the door clicked, walked inside and up the first landing.

He saw the second door on his right open a crack. When he headed that way, it swung open completely.

"Carter?"

"Yeah. Purdue?"

"Come in."

She was all legs holding up the kind of body you saw on movie screens. Her face was sharply aristocratic under a mane of dark brown hair. Her eyes were green, gold-flecked, and her mouth was just a touch too wide if you liked slide-rule symmetry.

All in all, she seemed lively, sensual, and very feminine. She also had an aura of superciliousness that hovered about her like a cloud.

"It's a two-bedroom flat. You can use that one."

Carter dropped his bag in the room and returned. "When do we meet Sir Charles Martin?"

"Tonight, eight. He has a house outside of Basingstoke, near Sherborne St. John."

"Good. Do you have a drink?"

Her left eyebrow shot up. Way up. "It's seven-thirty in the morning."

"I've got a watch. Scotch, if you have it."

He peeled out of his jacket and tie as she splashed whiskey into a glass.

"Here you are."

"Thanks."

"I don't like to work with drunks," she said coolly. "Do you drink a lot?"

"Only when I'm working."

"I don't think I like you."

"You don't have to like me to work with me," he replied. "I understand you work very closely with MI6, Sir Phillip Avery?"

"That's right."

"I've had dealings with Sir Phillip, and I think he's a dull-witted pompous ass. That should tell you how much I think of working with you. Where's the shower?"

When Carter emerged, a towel around his waist, she was standing at the foot of his bed.

"I've just had a call from Central."

"And?" Carter said, liking her more when she didn't

blink at his dropping the towel and pulling on a pair of shorts.

"Sir Charles just received another threat from Cory Howard."

"What's this one?"

"If Sir Charles doesn't pay the extortion money in seven days, acting as his own courier, Howard will kill him."

Carter frowned. *Maybe,* he thought, *Cory Howard has slipped a cog.*

FOUR

Sharon Purdue's car was a sleek gray Jaguar, a recent model with all the little luxury knickknacks money could buy. Carter noticed that it sported only a little over four thousand miles on the odometer as he slid into the soft leather seat.

"A rich daddy?" he asked drily.

She didn't reply but roared the powerful engine through the gears. It seemed only minutes before they were leaving London behind.

The woman made no effort at conversation and neither did Carter. He relaxed into the luxurious leather cushion of the passenger seat and stared broodingly at the darkening English countryside. The motorway was jammed with cars and trucks, but they reached the Basingstoke exit well before seven.

"Pub grub," Carter said suddenly.

"What?"

"I'm hungry. We've time, find a pub."

Over a meat pie and two pints of Courage, Carter thought about the dossier he had consumed on the plane.

Sir Charles Martin, the man he was about to meet, was as mysterious as he was wealthy. His wealth—wildly guessed at by British and American publications—was in the billion-pound range. Many thought even that figure was a low guess.

Just after the war, at the age of twenty, Sir Charles had taken over the family's small petrochemical plant near Dorset. In a short time he had expanded into other countries and steel mills and mining leases.

By 1975, he had so many companies under so many corporations that stock market followers couldn't really assess what he did own.

It was about that time when Sir Charles dropped out of public sight, preferring to be the master behind the scenes pulling his worldwide strings.

"It's getting late."

"What? Oh, yes. Sorry."

Carter paid, over her protests, and they returned to the car. The rest of the journey was completed over narrow, hedgerow-lined country lanes, and she drove with much more care and caution.

Presently she slowed to a crawl and turned into a lane between two stone pillars sporting rampaging lions at the top. "No guards?" Carter commented.

"This is only the outer wall. The estate is five hundred acres. The inner compound is about a mile ahead."

Carter whistled but said no more.

Sure enough, about five minutes later they pulled up to a set of massive iron-grilled gates. Two hard-eyed types appeared from a small house to the right. They wore bulky woolen sweaters, baggy trousers, and exhibited no arms, but Carter guessed from their look and movements that they could handle just about any situation.

After inspecting their credentials and making a call—evidently to another team of watchdogs in the house—Carter and Sharon were almost grudgingly waved through.

The road was graveled now, and it wound through a

forest of overhanging trees. Another hundred yards or so, and they turned into an open approach, a straight stretch flanked by rows of giant trees.

And then he saw it, an enormous Georgian manor at the end of the avenue. It had flanking wings the size of a normal palace, and its four stories were ablaze with lights. Just as they halted in front of a wide terrace, thunder ruptured the air and the rains came.

They both bolted for the door held open by a formally attired servant.

"I am Sharon Purdue and this is Mr. Nick Carter."

"Yes, miss, Sir Charles is in the study. This way, please."

Turning stiffly, he led them down a baronial hall. On either side, Carter saw stately rooms with enormous crystal chandeliers hanging fifteen feet above the floors. The floors themselves were littered with Persian and Bokhara carpets, slightly frayed but still glowing richly with color.

The study was lined with bookcases and gun racks. Heads of big game stared blankly down with glass eyes. Sir Charles rose from a huge wing chair in front of a massive fireplace and came to meet them.

"So glad you were able to just miss the storm. Sharon." He kissed her hand and turned to the Killmaster. "Mr. Carter."

"How do you do, Sir Charles."

The handshake was as firm as the man. Dressed in tailored tweeds with an ascot, he stood a good three inches taller than Carter and probably hit the scales at a solid 250.

Even more impressive than his size was his head. It looked too large even for the big body, and was topped by a mane of silver-streaked dark hair. The mustache on his strong upper lip was neatly trimmed, but his eyebrows hadn't seen scissors since birth.

"Please sit. Have you eaten? . . . A snack, perhaps?"

Carter's eyes drifted to the nearby food and liquor trolley. It was heaped with fresh and smoked salmon, Beluga caviar, cheeses, and a variety of sweets.

"No, thanks," Carter replied, "we had a meat pie in a pub."

Sharon Purdue glared. Sir Charles's blue eyes flashed with amusement and the full lips curled into a smile.

"I see. Pub food is . . . filling. A drink perhaps?"

When the sherry and scotch were poured, they settled in and Carter came right to the point.

"Could I see the two letters from Cory Howard, Sir Charles?"

"Of course."

He produced them with the envelopes, and Carter read:

Sir Charles: I think, sir, it is time you were brought to task. Of course, with your vast wealth and international connections, bringing you down to the level of the common man would be impossible. Therefore, I plan on making you pay another way. I want £5 million, in cash. Within 24 hours I want your agreement to pay. You can let me know by placing an ad in the personal column of the International Herald Tribune reading: "H. The sum is reasonable. M."

If you don't pay, I have enough evidence concerning your MI6 and CIA backstairs dealings to bring your secret empire down like a house of cards.

I think you know what I mean: Uruguay, Bolivia, Colombia, Canada.

And you needn't send any more amateurs. You can verify the enclosed with the French Sûreté. Howard.

The note was handwritten. Carter fished from his pocket the two examples he had of Howard's handwriting and compared them to the note.

They matched perfectly.

"What was enclosed, Sir Charles?"

"These."

The man passed over two passports, one Italian, the other French. The names were Guido Narboni and Jules Lafaye. The photographs on both passports had black *X*'s drawn through them.

"You knew these men, Sir Charles?"

"Not directly, no. I questioned my people in France and Italy. They were both private detectives. My firms had used them in the past as antiterrorist security consultants."

"And that was all?" Carter asked.

Sir Charles shrugged. "To my knowledge, yes."

"And did you check with the French?"

He fumbled with an unlit pipe and glanced at Sharon Purdue.

"Our office did," she said. "Both men were found in the Seine, murdered. One man had been shot twice in the heart from close range. The other man's neck was broken."

Carter paused to light a cigarette and gather his thoughts. "Sir Charles, just what 'backstairs dealings' do you think Howard is talking about?"

"Other than the intelligence gathering that I and several officers of my company have done in the past, I have no idea what the man is referring to."

"Do you have business dealings in the countries Howard mentions?"

The man smiled. "Of course. Mr. Carter, there are probably no more than four or five countries in the entire world in which I *don't* conduct some form of business."

Carter dragged deeply on his cigarette and let the exhaled smoke shield his eyes as he studied the dapper English gentleman across from him.

He was all he seemed to be, and unless he was an actor of the first order, it would appear he was telling the truth.

But Carter knew Cory Howard. The man didn't go off half-cocked. That is, unless the dangerous life he had been leading for years had finally driven him off the deep end.

Carter picked up the second note.

Sir Charles: So you've decided not to play. In a way, that's a pity. In another way, it isn't, since it gives me the moral latitude to apply more pressure and up the stakes.

It's £10 million now, plus a personal meeting. Be prepared to transfer the money and meet with me in 7 days' time. Acknowledgment will be the same way in the Paris Herald.

Be forewarned: if the ad is not placed in 7 days' time, all deals are off. I will not only turn over all the evidence I have to The New York Times and to the London Times, I will also go on the hunt . . . for you. Howard.

Sharon Purdue had previously read the initial extortion note. Carter handed her the second, and faced Sir Charles.

"If Cory Howard is serious, your life could be in grave danger, Sir Charles. He is good at what he does, perhaps the best."

The older man shrugged and smiled. "This is not the first threat on my life. Besides, Sir Phillip Avery tells me that you, Mr. Carter, are the best in this business."

"Perhaps, but I am not in the bodyguard business. What do you want us to do?"

"Find Cory Howard. If he can somehow substantiate these claims, then perhaps there is some skullduggery in my companies that I don't know about. If that is the case, then I will agree to meet with him."

"But you don't want to pay."

"Of course not. If I paid every extortion demand I've

received through the years, I would be lucky to afford a magazine kiosk in Trafalgar Square."

"Very well," Carter sighed. "Of course I'll have to confer with Washington, but I'm sure I'll get the go-ahead. I can't speak for MI6."

Sharon Purdue handed the note back to Sir Charles. "Sir Phillip has already agreed to my participation."

The Killmaster made a wry face. He could see the advantages of bringing this woman into it because of how much she could add about Howard. But that didn't mean he would enjoy working with her haughty, acerbic personality. Also, if the going got rough, he would rather be backed up by an experienced field agent rather than someone lifted from a foreign intelligence desk.

"I'd like to take those two letters and the envelopes with me," he said. "Analyzing the paper may give us a source and general location on Howard." The man hesitated. Carter thought he knew why. "They will be well cared for, I assure you."

The letters and both envelopes were handed over. Carter pocketed them and stood.

"I want to make something clear, Sir Charles . . ."

"Of course."

"I've worked closely with Howard in the past. At times I found him a little too eager to resort to violence in many situations, and often he made impetuous decisions in the execution of a mission. But always I found him ethical and scrupulously honest. I'll find Howard, but before I'll turn him over to anyone else, I'll find out what in God's name drove him to attempt anything as petty as extortion."

"Please do, Mr. Carter. And I give you my word that, if Howard does have any incriminating evidence against any of my employees, I swear to you that I will get to the bottom of it and root it out."

Sir Charles himself saw them to the car. Just before

sliding into the Jag, Carter turned to the man and asked one last question.

"Just what is your prime business, Sir Charles, in the countries Howard mentioned?"

"Why, mostly strategic minerals. We have several mining leases there, and leases on other properties that are about to be developed."

"Just what kind of minerals?"

The older man took a deep breath and concentrated. "Practically all of them, in one form or another—chromium, uranium, cobalt, manganese, vanadium . . . the list could go on for pages."

"Thank you, Sir Charles. We'll be in touch." Carter turned to Sharon. "Let's go."

The woman turned the car around, and minutes later they were through the guarded gate.

"What do you think?" she asked.

"Right now, very little."

"Back to London?"

"I don't think so," Carter replied. "Did you notice the postmarks on those envelopes?"

She nodded. "Treyarnon."

"Where is that?"

"On the west coast of Cornwall, north of Newquay. You don't think Cory is actually in England . . . that he mailed those himself . . ."

"Of course not, but he has a house somewhere in Cornwall, and I'm sure he probably has many friends who could have done the forward mailing for him."

"The house is on a cliff overlooking the ocean just outside the village of Treyarnon."

Carter's head swiveled around sharply, his eyes studying her profile in the dim lights from the dash. "I take it you've been there?"

Even in the dim light he could see a flush creeping up her face. "I have, several times."

"Just how close were you to Cory Howard?"

"We were good friends."

"How good?"

"Damn you," she hissed, "you know, so why do you ask?"

"I'd like to hear your version."

"We were lovers off and on for about a year, right after he left the agency. He tried to recruit me to work for him. I didn't do it."

"Why not?"

"Let's just say I didn't approve of his methods, and I think what he does is better left to the authorities."

"Oh. Is that why you broke up?"

"We didn't 'break up,' as you put it. We just drifted apart, as people do." Suddenly the car lurched to a halt. "Which way, left or right?"

"What's left?"

"London."

"That means Cornwall is right. Go right!"

"We won't get back to London before morning."

"They have hotels in Cornwall," Carter rasped, crawling over the seat into the back. "I'll buy you clean underwear and a toothbrush. Wake me when we get there."

"Damn," he heard her hiss as the car lurched forward and screamed through the gears.

FIVE

After a brief stop in Newquay to make sure they had lodging for the night, they drove on north the short distance to Treyarnon. Two miles past the village, Sharon cut down a winding lane toward the sea.

"We'll have to walk from here."

"Any houses close by?"

"Not close enough to see a light," she replied, switching on a flash and guiding Carter toward the sound of the sea.

Minutes later, they came to the cliff edge and turned right toward Howard's house. Actually, it was little more than a two-story, half-timbered cottage with a thatched roof. Around it was a small stone fence. Over the fence, in carefully manicured gardens, Carter took the lead.

"Everything's been kept up."

"There's a caretaker from the village. He doubles as a gardener. Are you going to break in?"

"If I have to," Carter said, making a complete tour of the house and ending at the rear, at a kitchen door that faced the sea. "But I won't have to."

He played the flash down the door. The sill near the lock had been shattered.

Carter filled his left hand with Wilhelmina and went through the door, hard.

The interior was as quiet as a church. And it was messy

as a junkyard. Cabinets had been pulled from the walls as well as the dining alcove. Pots, pans, and broken dishes littered the floor.

"It's clear," he hissed. "Come on in."

Sharon joined him, and gasped. "My God."

The dining room, study, and great room were in the same condition.

"Your people?" Carter asked.

"Certainly not. Sir Phillip didn't want to bring any MI6 or MI5 people in, for fear of blowing Sir Charles. That's why only you and I are involved."

"Wait here."

Carter returned to the kitchen. He flashed his light across the floor until he found a pair of rubber gloves he had spotted earlier.

"Here, put one of these on. Don't touch anything with your ungloved hand."

It took an hour to go through the trash on the floor and then the strewn contents of the desk in the study.

Nothing.

"Howard surely kept files somewhere."

"There's a wall safe," Sharon replied. "The upper master bedroom."

She led the way, and then stopped cold in the center of the doorway. Carter moved her aside and stepped in, lifting the flash from her hand.

He was short, with a heavy body, a shaggy mane of dark, graying hair, and a last-generation British mustache. In life he must have had the look of a charging water buffalo.

In death he just looked like a worn-out old man.

"It's the caretaker," Sharon said. "His name is Argus, or something like that."

"His name *was* Argus," Carter growled, crossing the room.

A little gentle probing told him that the man had been dead for about eight hours. Further searching revealed no wounds of any kind.

He wore a heavy woolen shirt under a worse-for-wear windbreaker and tweedy trousers. His boots were the heavy hiking kind, and they were muddy.

But there was no mud on the carpet and very little on the bed.

"My guess is he died downstairs and was carried up here."

"Was he killed?"

Carter shook his head. "Don't think so. My guess is a heart attack, probably downstairs, and they carried him up here."

He played the light across the wall until it fell on the safe, the small round door hanging from half a hinge.

It was empty.

Gingerly he played the light inside until he found the manufacturer's plate: Orcron, Geneva, Model 82401.

Carter concentrated, going back through the data bank in his mind until he had it: five-digit combination, two tumbler, with an added number after the first tumbler was released.

A very hard safe to crack, and time-consuming. They hadn't bothered. They had merely drilled the door and blown it.

Whoever had trashed Howard's place had been thorough, and probably fast. And it had been a team, not one or two men.

"Argus there," Carter said, "did he live alone?"

"Yes. He was a widower."

"Good. It will be a while before he's missed. We can stay at Newquay safely for the night. Let's go. I'm tired."

In the car, Sharon asked, "That old man . . ."

"Yeah?"

"Finding him dead didn't bother you, did it?"

"No. Everybody dies." To his surprise she smiled. "Something?"

"Not really. I was just thinking you're the perfect one to find Cory Howard."

It was three in the morning by the time they got to the hotel. Carter chuckled when he found the key in the door.

Just like the English. Must lock up at precisely twelve, but, never fear, the key is there!

The desk, with the key boxes behind it, was directly in front of them. To the left was the door to the pub, closed, of course. To the right, past an open pay phone, the stairs went up and then back around practically over their heads.

Carter leaned across the desk, got their room keys, and led the way up the stairs.

At her door, Carter lifted a mini-bottle of scotch from his coat pocket. "Care for a nightcap?"

"Oh, God, no," Sharon groaned. "I'm completely bushed, out on my feet."

"Suit yourself."

He was just unlocking his door when she called to him. "Nick . . ."

"Yeah?"

"If I've been a little brusque, short, I hope you'll forgive me. I've never been assigned to chase one of our own before."

Carter grinned. "Just think of it as chasing an old boyfriend."

In the room, he made all the nighttime noises for retiring. He left his trousers on as he popped the mini-bottle and stretched across the bed.

He had just finished his scotch, when he sensed—as much as heard—her door gently open. He waited until he was sure she was gone, and then moved into the hall himself, leaving his door open behind him.

On the balls of his feet and in a crouch, he moved down the hall until he was on the landing directly above the pay phone. He heard her giving the local operator the number, but couldn't catch it. He was able to hear every whispered word when her party came on the line at last.

"We're in Newquay, at a hotel... after leaving Sir Charles, Carter wanted to go through Howard's house... yes, it was a shambles... and that's not all. We found the caretaker dead... Carter didn't seem to think so, maybe a heart attack... no, I'm sure of it. Neither of us found anything. I watched him all the time... seven in the morning..."

The Killmaster didn't wait for the rest of it. He padded back to his room, undressed, and slipped into bed.

As he dozed off, the thought slid back and forth in his mind that, from here on in, everything Little Miss Muffin Purdue knew, Sir Phillip Avery would know. And if Avery knew, then Carter guessed Sir Charles Martin would know soon after.

That is, if it were Sir Phillip that she had called.

Over breakfast and the early-morning drive back to London, Sharon Purdue was downright chummy. That is, until Carter had her pull over on Park Lane near the Dorchester.

"What's this about?" she asked.

"No sense both of us doing the same thing and covering the same ground. We're splitting up." He handed her the letters and the two envelopes. "You must have a connection or two at Scotland Yard."

"Yes, but—"

"Get these analyzed. It's a long shot, but if we can locate the manufacturer, we might also get a general area on the retailer."

"Of course I can follow that up. But what are you going to do?"

Carter was already out of the car. "Sightsee," he announced, and grinned. "It's a beautiful day."

Her eyes were flashing indignation and frustration, but she had little choice. From a nearby kiosk, glancing over newspaper headlines, he watched her pull away and disappear in traffic.

He turned north and strolled into the Dorchester Hotel. He gave the woman at the telephone exchange Hawk's hotline number for field agents, and took a seat in the booth she specified to wait for the overseas connection to be completed.

"Yes?" came the cigar-gruff voice.

The Killmaster waited until he was sure the operator had disconnected before he spoke. "N3."

"What have you got?"

"The extortion demand is for real. At least it's in Howard's handwriting." He repeated almost word for word the contents of both notes. "Either Cory Howard is on to something big about Sir Charles, or he's decided he needs some funds for early retirement."

"I doubt the latter," Hawk growled. "I had a long talk with John Starkey and Burt Esterman. I didn't mention Sir Charles by name, but I got out of them the fact that John Hutchins did have an English source for class-A stuff. Has had for quite a while."

"So that intelligence could be coming from Sir Charles through Sir Phillip Avery at MI6?"

"Could, probably is. I traced a few items that I got from Starkey, and they fit the locations where Sir Charles has a lot of business interests."

"At least we're on solid ground there," Carter said. "But someone else is looking for Howard, and not so delicately."

"What do you mean?"

Carter told him about going through Howard's house in Cornwall and what they had found. "But I'm sure the old man died a natural death."

"Sounds like MI6."

"Purdue says positively not," Carter replied. "My guess is Sir Charles himself. Let's face it, with his money and clout he's probably got an army at his disposal."

"Then watch yourself," Hawk said. "Too many fingers in the pie and you could end up in the middle. Anything else?"

"Yeah, as much as you can get me on a pair named Guido Narboni and Jules Lafaye, one out of Paris, one out of Rome. Supposed to be two private investigators with antiterrorist specialties."

"Any particular reason?"

"Yeah. I think Howard wasted them and dumped them in the Seine. I'll keep in touch."

Carter hung up and left the hotel. He walked down Park Lane, turned left at Curzon, and five minutes later stood in front of the building housing Lilly Kalensky's Mayfair flat.

It was posh, with a lot of marble in the lobby and a uniformed doorman. Carter moved inside, fishing a card from a stack he always kept on hand.

"Good day, sir."

"And good day to you," Carter said in a clipped Oxford accent. "I'm redoing Miss Kalensky's boudoir. I have a key."

The doorman frowned over the card: DWIGHT BRAXTON INTERIORS, KING'S ROAD, CHELSEA.

"You are Mr. Braxton, sir?"

"I am," Carter replied, scanning the mailboxes until he spotted Lilly's name.

"I don't see your name on the visitors' list, sir, and Miss Kalensky left no instructions—"

"That's because she expected to be back by now. Office got a call from her on Cayman Brac yesterday. We could call her, but I really don't have the time. Miss Kalensky is most anxious that the work be completed as quickly as possible." He was already heading toward the elevators. "You needn't bother showing me up, I know the way . . . Two-B."

The elevator closed on a shrugging doorman and Carter stepped out on the second floor with his picks already in hand.

The lock was a standard spring release on the bottom and a two-tumbler deadbolt on top. It took ten seconds to open it, and Carter moved into the opulent sunken living room.

Whatever it was Lilly Kalensky did for Cory Howard besides sleeping with him, she was well paid for it.

To his right, through the open door, he saw a lavishly appointed bedroom full of fine English antiques. To his left, through a thirteen-foot arch, was a formal, walnut-paneled dining room with a main table that would seat twelve. Along the wall were two solid oak sideboards laden with crystal and silver.

The living room itself sported Moroccan carpets over highly polished wood floors reflecting the glow of rich velvet draperies. A massive marble fireplace dominated one wall.

It was luxurious, expensive, neat as a pin, and hardly lived in.

The kitchen, dining room, and living room yielded nothing to his search. Rack after rack of expensive clothes in the bedroom closet reinforced Lilly's worth.

The last thing he attacked was a desk in an alcove off the bedroom. The desk revealed nothing either, until he picked a locked drawer at the very bottom. Inside, he found stocks, bonds, gold certificates, and three bankbooks from the Bank of England, Cayman National, and Banque Suisse, Geneva.

Idly, Carter totaled it all up and chuckled. A little over two million pounds. Not bad for a little Hungarian refugee.

It also told him something else. If Lilly Kalensky worked for Cory Howard and was worth this kind of money, then what was Howard himself worth?

Too much, Carter guessed, to resort to extortion.

In the bottom of the drawer under everything else, he found two wills. One was Lilly's, the other a copy of Cory Howard's. Both named Jova Kalen as their sole beneficiary. They were drawn up by a lawyer in the Caymans, one Arnold Kingsley.

Carter copied down the address, replaced everything in the drawer, and locked it.

The last thing he did was rewind the tape on her answering machine and replay it.

There were three messages: one from a dental secretary confirming an appointment, a second from a dry cleaners, and the last from Cory Howard.

"Lilly, this is Cory. I'm afraid you'll have to cancel the visit to Jova. We have a bit of business for StarFire in Paris. Meet me in Buenos Aires day after tomorrow. Also, phone Otto and tell him I'll need connections for hardware there. Love you."

Carter killed the tape and erased it. It took him fifteen minutes rifling through the Roladex on the desk before he found the name and address: Otto Luderman, 16 Cormel, Paddington.

He dialed Otto's number.

"*Ja?*"

Carter hung up and left the apartment.

It was a crumbling old tenement. The entire area was ancient, decayed with time and the foul air from nearby factories. Old men, probably pensioners, lounged against the rusted iron railings around the stoops. Pakistani and Indian children played in the streets. On the corner, a gang of boys—dark-skinned, long-haired, and leather-jacketed —sized Carter up for a mugging.

A nearby window was open, and the sound of guitar music and a falsetto voice extolling the virtues of kinky sex filled the street.

Inside, a nauseating odor greeted him. He checked the mailboxes until he found Otto Luderman's name. Four flights up he paused at a battered door and knocked.

"Hallo, darlink!" a raspy voice said. "Come in and sit, if you can find a place!"

The apartment was a shambles. It carried the odor of unwashed bodies, greasy food, and resembled an unprofitable antique shop. A mantelpiece, painted pea-soup green, sported a picture of King George and a bad porcelain copy of the Winged Victory. The ceiling was flaking, each corner occupied by a family of industrious spiders. There was a rug on the floor, but it was probably stolen from some theater. Its edges were ragged and its surface showed the result of many marching feet.

In the middle of it all sat a small man in tweedy cast-offs, with a once-slender body that was now going to fat. He had the broad, sloping shoulders of a working man, and a deeply lined face with dark, opaque eyes and a misshapen, many-times-broken nose.

"Otto Luderman?" Carter asked, lighting a cigarette to kill the smell.

"*Ja* . . . who . . . ?"

"Nick Carter. If that's a weapon you're reaching for, don't. I'll break your arm before you can use it."

"What you want wid me?" the man said, the hand snapping back to fidget with its twin in his lap.

"I want to know how you contact Cory Howard." He sat

down on a tacky velvet love seat that immediately belched
a cloud of dust.

"Don't know the name."

"I'm going to be patient for two minutes, Otto, then I'm
going to start breaking bones in different parts of your
body."

The hard eyes squinted. "You a copper?"

"No, a friend of Howard's. A while back, you set up an
arms buy for Howard and Lilly Kalensky in Buenos
Aires."

"You fulla shit!"

Carter moved like a striking cobra. He grabbed a nearby
empty wine bottle with his right hand and snapped the neck
off on the edge of a trunk. At the same time, he snatched
Luderman's wrist with his left hand and brought it smashing down, palm up, on the trunk.

"How do you contact Howard?" he said calmly, easing
the jagged neck of the bottle into the man's palm.

Luderman squealed and sweated, but he still held out.
"Cory a bad sombitch. You hurt me, I think he *kill* me."

Carter turned the bottle. Luderman screamed and
reached for it with his free hand. The Killmaster sliced the
free hand twice in a blurring movement, and brought it
back to the stationary palm with double the previous pressure.

"Howard isn't here, Otto, I am. And you're going to
wish I killed you if you don't talk."

"Oh, Blessed Jesus . . ."

"He can't help you either. How, Otto?"

"Two ways . . . let go, let go!"

Carter released the hand, tossed the bottle away, and
leaned back. "I'm listening. Two ways, you said?"

"When he has work for me, I get a call, long distance. I
don't know from where."

"Howard?"

"No. Some guy, Brit accent. He always says, 'This is AK,' then tells me what Howard needs and where. If I can do it, he tells me a price and that's it."

That would be Arnold Kingsley, Carter thought. "Was that the procedure on the Buenos Aires deal?"

"No, that time a woman called to give me the go-ahead."

"Did you know her?"

"No, but I knew the voice. She was always the one who made the payoffs for Howard. So I went ahead."

"Good, Otto. Now, how did you contact him when you had to?"

"A number in Cornwall, somebody named Argus . . . an old man's voice. I'd call, and an hour later Howard or this AK would call me here."

"Damn," Carter hissed.

"That's it, I swear!"

"Yeah, I believe you," Carter said, standing and heading for the door. "You'd better get to a doctor, Otto . . . that's a nasty cut you've got."

"Bastard!"

"And, Otto, if you hear from this AK again, tell him I'm coming. Don't forget the name. Carter, Nick Carter."

On the street, he hailed a cab and gave the driver Sharon Purdue's address.

She was waiting, a sherry in her hand and a packed bag at her feet.

"Going somewhere?"

"Just getting prepared," she shrugged. "I figure we'll be going somewhere eventually."

"How did you do?"

"Paper and envelopes both manufactured in Lyon, France. Ninety-five percent of their output is sold in Paris. Any good?"

"I doubt it. Probably another dead end. Howard might

have mailed the first note from Paris to Argus for remailing, but I think he was long gone from France before he mailed the second."

"Your office called the Center here; they put it through to me. They want you to call as soon as possible."

For the second time that day, Carter called the hot-line number. Hawk answered on the first ring.

"It's me."

"Are you sitting down?" Hawk growled.

"Should I be?"

"I think so. Interpol wired an hour ago. They found a woman's body five days ago outside Buenos Aires in a shallow grave. Just identified her this morning."

"Lilly Kalensky."

"You guessed it. The Buenos Aires police traced her back to the El Conquistador Hotel. She was registered along with Cory Howard. They have an Interpol-Want out for Howard, first-degree murder."

"I'll call you from the Cayman Islands."

"You do that," Hawk said, and hung up.

Carter had barely replaced the phone when Sharon picked it up, the model of efficiency.

"I'll book us reservations on the first available flight."

SIX

The only connection was a British Airways flight to Miami and Cayman Airways to the islands. It was a little after three in the afternoon when they touched down at Owen Roberts Airport on Grand Cayman.

As they moved through customs, Carter sensed, rather than saw, the watchers. Three quick glances checking the time on a wall clock or looking for the rental car counter identified them.

Miles Proctor, MI6, sat in an open bar toying with a drink and scanning every disembarking passenger. There was a short, rotund man perusing paperbacks at the newsstand. Carter couldn't put a name to him, but he knew the face. He was a low-level CIA fieldman. The third one sat smoking a pipe in the arrival area with a newspaper in front of his face. He was Arkady Svetov, KGB.

Carter knew him well, and knew that Svetov knew him. He figured that all three of them would.

He couldn't suppress a low chuckle. All three cruised the Caribbean, including the Bahamas and Bermuda. Ninety-nine percent of what they did was spy on each other.

The Caribbean was a dumping ground for over-the-hill

fieldmen. In the islands they could feel that they were still contributing, while actually they were enjoying preretirement retirement.

"Something?" Sharon asked, carrying her own bag as they headed for the Avis counter.

"Not really," Carter replied a little too loudly. "Just thinking what a wonderful vacation we're going to have."

The car was a four-door Escort with the drive on the right side.

"I hate driving on the wrong side. You drive," he growled.

She glared, but drove. The capital of George Town was a pretty little village with older, well-restored buildings and rainbow-colored houses mixed in with the more modern, concrete-and-glass structures. At the harbor, Carter told her to turn right.

"Ever been to Cayman?"

"No," she replied. "It's lovely. Too bad we can't really be on holiday."

"Yeah. Turn in here."

It was the Tamarind Bay Hotel, very expensive and very posh. She said as much.

"One of the perks of the job," he chuckled.

With a little urging and his diplomatic VIP passport, they got a two-bedroom villa with a terrace overlooking the white sand beach and incredibly blue, crystal-clear ocean.

"Will there be anything else, sir?"

"No, that's fine," Carter said. He tipped the bellman and built two drinks at the mini-bar. Then he took them, the telephone, and the island directory out to the veranda. Sharon Purdue was already there taking in the magnificent view.

"This is paradise," she murmured.

Carter nodded and handed her a drink. "It is, and they even have a couple of growth industries besides tourism."

"What do they grow?"

"Banks and turtles. You'd better change."

"Into a bathing suit?"

"Well, I'll be damned," he said drily, "you're being coy. No, a pair of slacks and walking shoes. You're going for a boat ride."

"Where to?"

"Cayman Brac. Lilly Kalensky has a villa there. My guess is that her younger sister will be there. I want you to interrogate her further than I have, and get her permission to go over the house."

"Will she let me?"

"She will if you use my name."

"What will I be looking for?"

"Damned if I know."

Sharon went inside with a resigned shrug, and Carter hit the directory.

There was no listing for Lilly Kalensky on Cayman Brac, but he hadn't expected to find one. There were two listings for Arnold Kingsley, his George Town office and his home in the West Bay area.

Carter called the office number first.

"I'm sorry, but Mr. Kingsley has left the office."

"Where can I reach him?"

"Is this an emergency?"

"Yeah."

A little hesitation. "He might be at his residence . . ."

Carter hung up and redialed. A woman answered.

"Is this the Kingsley residence?"

"Yes, this is Mrs. Kingsley."

"I'd like to speak to your husband, Mrs. Kingsley."

"I'm sorry, he can't be disturbed."

"I think he can. Tell him it's Otto Luderman."

A male voice laced with anger and a touch of fright popped in at once. He had probably been on an extension.

"I'll take it, Leona." There was a click and Kingsley spoke again. "Who the hell is this?"

"My name is Nick Carter. I want to talk to you, but not at your home or office."

"How do you know Otto Luderman?"

"Never mind. I'm a friend of a friend. It's him I want to talk about. Where can we meet?"

He still hesitated. "I've been with the police all day. Are you the police?"

So, Carter thought, *the cogs of the law have swung into gear*. He decided one last jolt would do it.

"Does Jova know about her sister?"

There was a long pause and then a tentative "Yes."

"Is she here?"

"Yes, she arrived around noon from New York. You know Jova?"

"Yeah. Call her and mention my name. Then call me back."

He clicked off the hotel number and the extension, and hung up. The phone rang before Carter had sat back down from building a second drink.

"Yeah?"

"There is a bar across from Safe Harbor called Corky's. I'll be there in an hour."

"I'll be there," Carter replied. "Is Jova on Cayman Brac?"

"Yes."

"Call her again. Tell her she's going to get a visitor, a woman. Her name is Sharon Purdue. Tell Jova she can trust this woman."

"Can she?" There was real concern in his voice.

"She can. I'll see you in an hour, Kingsley."

One last call and he had the ferry schedule to Cayman Brac. One left in twenty minutes.

"I'm ready."

"Then let's go."

As they drove into George Town and the ferry pier, Carter gave Sharon a rundown on Jova Kalen.

"Go easy on the girl. She didn't know the kind of business her sister was in. But be firm enough so she'll let you go through Lilly's things."

Sharon nodded. At the pier she got out of the car and leaned back in the window. "I looked it up. It's sixty miles over there. I probably won't be back tonight."

"That may be for the better," Carter replied. "I imagine Jova could use a shoulder to cry on."

"You won't run off without me, will you?"

Carter grinned. "Why, would you miss me?"

He drove off, watching her smolder in the rearview mirror.

Corky's was a typical island hangout for the locals, with hanging baskets, lots of greenery, dark wood inside, and wicker tables and chairs in an outside patio.

There were a few tourists mixed in with the locals, but not many. Carter could see why Kingsley had chosen the place. He would be easy for the lawyer to spot.

Carter sat at one of the patio tables and ordered a beer. When it came, he lit a cigarette and waited.

On the hour exactly, a tall blond man with athletic shoulders and powerful arms came through the door. He paused at the bar, got a beer, and headed directly to Carter's table.

He was burned almost black by the sun, and dressed in white duck pants, sandals, a gaily striped cotton shirt open over his hefty chest, and a battered canvas hat.

"Carter?"

"Yeah, sit down."

He regarded the Killmaster with a partly insolent, partly tolerant, mostly appraising look, then sat.

"Who are you, exactly?"

"Kind of a cross between St. Jude and De Sade," Carter replied, shoving his credentials across the table.

Kingsley looked, let his eyes widen a bit, and, after pushing the wallet back to Carter, rubbed nervous fingers against his temples.

"Christ, the government. What do you want with me?"

"You should know. Cory Howard."

The head came up. "Cory didn't murder Lilly Kalensky. He couldn't."

"I don't think he did either. But that's not why I want to talk to him."

"Well . . . ?"

Carter ignored that for the time being. "You handle all of Cory's affairs?"

"No, just his personal stuff, investments, things like that."

"You don't handle the Salvation Limited legal work?"

"No. There's a firm in London that handles that: Shroeder, Caen and Adams, Bond Street. I have nothing to do with Cory's professional life."

"Oh? Then why do you make contacts for Cory with people like Otto Luderman?"

The tan lightened by about two shades and his knuckles went white around the beer bottle. "I do that because most of the time the . . . items . . ."

"Guns, plastique, grenades?"

Kingsley swallowed. "Yes. They are, of course, illegal. So Cory doesn't want the payment for them to come out of Salvation accounts. It's a strictly legit company. I pay out of his personal accounts here on Cayman through money transfers."

"So it can't be traced?"

"Yes."

"How do you get in touch with him?"

"I don't."

"Bullshit," Carter hissed.

"I don't, I swear it." Suddenly the macho voice developed a little squeak. "God, Cory hardly lights anywhere. He's all over the world. He contacts me."

Carter leaned forward, lowering his voice even more. "I've worked with Howard. I know how thorough he is . . . that's how he's stayed alive. He has angles for everything. There are always emergencies."

Kingsley was sweating now, his shirt soaking through. Carter laid the two notes in front of him and covered Sir Charles Martin's name with his fingers.

The other man read them and looked up, sheer shock spreading across his face. "Extortion? . . . Cory?"

"That's Howard's handwriting, isn't it?"

"Yes," he said, nodding glumly.

"You're positive?"

"Of course. I deal with something he's written almost every day. Look, Cory isn't exactly a saint. His methods sometimes frighten the hell out of me. But extortion?— Never!"

"I don't think so either," Carter admitted. "Let me tell you something, Kingsley. He's playing with the big boys now, very sticky stuff. I've got to talk to him and find out why before they get very pissed."

There was a lot of temple rubbing and some lip biting. Finally a shiver ran through the man's body and he nodded.

"All right, there is a way. But it will take a little time."

"It can't, not over twenty-four hours. You know where to reach me."

Carter dropped some bills on the table and stood. Kingsley grabbed his elbow as he went by.

"Wait . . ."

"Yeah?"

"What should I tell him, I mean, specifically, to convince him? Cory is not a very trusting guy."

"Just give him my name and set up a meet."

Kingsley chuckled and shook his head. "You think that's going to be enough for Cory?"

Carter leaned over until his nose was practically touching the other man's. "Okay, tell him that, if he doesn't agree to a meet, then I'll have to come after him. And if I do that, I have to consider him a rogue. He'll know what that means."

Leaving the lawyer clutching his beer, he went out into the gathering dusk.

Carter froze when he saw the back of the man's head above the side window of the Escort. Then he saw the wreath of smoke, and relaxed.

"Hello, Arkady," Carter said, slipping into the driver's seat.

"Nicholas! I can't tell you how surprised I was to see you arriving in this backwater part of the world." His English was perfect, with a Cambridge lilt. He had learned it at the KGB language school in Kiev and polished it at the Military Diplomatic Academy in Moscow.

"Just taking a little vacation," Carter said with a grin.

"Oh, please don't say that, Nicholas," he groaned. "Do you realize I haven't sent in a decent report in months? The least you could do is give me some tidbit so Moscow will keep paying my bills."

Carter laughed out loud. "You don't need tidbits anymore, Arkady. You should be up for retirement soon."

The man's gray face screwed itself into a grimace. "God, don't say that! If I retire, I'll have to go back to the Ukraine and snow and my wife!"

"Didn't know you were a family man, Arkady."

"I'm not . . . you haven't seen my wife. Speaking of

women, who's the bird?"

Carter shrugged. "Met her in London. Liked what I saw, so I asked her to come on vacation with me."

"You're not being very cooperative."

Carter laughed again. "How'd you follow me out? Taxi?"

Svetov nodded and Carter started the car. "I'll give you a lift back to town."

"Good of you."

They swapped war stories and other lies as Carter drove back to George Town. The Killmaster stopped across from the marine loading pier to let Svetov off.

"There's a good place for dinner right near here called Borshov's. They make me special dishes. Buy you dinner?"

Carter shook his head. "My 'bird' wanted a look at Cayman Brac. She won't be back tonight, so I think I'll fancy a little solo night life," he replied with a leering smile.

"There's damned little around here," the Russian said as he hauled his bulk from the car.

"I've heard of a place run by a woman named Rita Lyon. Know it?"

Arkady Svetov nodded. "That would be the Seaside. Just follow South Church Street. Beyond Ambassador's Inn, make a right to the shore. It's right there."

"Thanks."

"Uh, Nicholas . . ."

"Yeah?"

"Would you mind if I put in my report that you're down here checking me out? It would boost my importance rating several points."

"Sure thing," Carter said, laughing. "Anything for a friend."

"Cheerio, Nicholas."

"Cheerio, Arkady."

Carter followed the Russian's directions and pulled into the lot in front of a one-story blue stucco building. It was early, so there were only a couple of other cars in the lot.

The inside was almost a replica of Corky's, with the hanging baskets being replaced by oars, hanging seashells, and a few life preservers on the walls.

The customers consisted of a couple of local fishermen and a tourist couple trying to recapture the magic of the honeymoon they'd taken twenty years before.

"Hey, babee, what you have?"

The bartender was a young Sammy Davis, Jr., complete with cool black glasses and a ton of gold.

"Beer."

"Right on."

Carter dropped two Cayman twenties on the bar when the beer came. "Is Rita around?"

"Naw, she don't make the scene until about eight. Sometimes she don't come in at all on a weeknight. Just sits in her bungalow and watches telly."

"Could you call her up and tell her a friend of an old friend would like to say hello?"

"Sure thing."

"Thanks. You got food?"

"Hell, yes, man!"

"Order me up something, keep the beer coming, and the change is yours."

"Sheeeit."

Carter spotted a pay phone near the rest rooms and called the hotel.

"Yes, sir, there was one call, a lady. She left a number."

Carter memorized it, cut the connection, and dialed. Sharon Purdue answered on the third ring.

"How goes it?"

"Fine, we're fast friends already . . . and right now she

needs one. You're right—she's a nice girl."

"Yeah, I know. Find anything yet?"

"I just started looking. Can you give me a hint?"

"Phone numbers, addresses . . . anything that might have something to do with Howard. Before this evening is over, I should have at least two people getting word to him that I want to talk, but we'll still keep digging."

"All right. I won't be back tonight."

"No problem. Has Jova been pumping you?"

"Yes, incessantly, but I've managed to be vague."

"Good, keep it that way. See you tomorrow."

His food was waiting at the bar when he returned, a jumbo seafood platter and a fresh beer. He was just pushing the empty platter away when a woman slid onto the stool beside him.

"You want to see Rita, darling?"

She was a wiry woman caressing forty, with sun-bleached blond hair and skin burned to the color of mahogany. The accent was French, and it seemed to match the simple, off-the-shoulder blouse in deep red and the full-cut, multihued skirt.

"You're Rita?"

"What did you expect, a sweet young thing?" The laugh was low and husky, but not sultry.

"My name's Carter. I'm a friend of Lilly Kalensky and her little sister."

He watched the eyes narrow slightly, but other than that, there was no change in her expression. If anything, the wide smile grew wider.

She didn't know.

"Lilly is a good woman. She help me buy this place."

"When was the last time you saw Lilly?"

Now the smile faded. "Why you want to know? You sure you Lilly's friend?"

"Rita, Lilly's dead."

The eyes grew dull, the face paled, and both hands clutched the bar. "No, cannot be!"

"She is dead. She was killed in Buenos Aires a few days ago. The police there think Cory Howard did it. I don't think so. I want to find Howard."

"You police?"

"No, I really am a friend. Jova is here now, at the villa on Cayman Brac."

Rita slid from the stool. "I must go to little girl!"

Carter grabbed her arm. "No need, I have someone with her. Is there somewhere we can talk?"

She hesitated, then nodded. "I think you have mean eyes but honest face. Come, I have bungalow in back, on beach."

In the rear of the club was a patio with a fountain in the center. From it a number of narrow paths went off into the foliage in several directions. The woman took one and Carter followed.

A hundred yards into the maze of hedges and flowers, they came to another patio. Carter followed her through a narrow doorway leading into the house from the patio. The bungalow was totally feminine, with lots of chintz and soft pastel colors.

Wordlessly, she motioned him to a sofa and poured herself a glass of rum and opened him a beer.

"To friends," she toasted, and drank the whole glass without blinking in three swallows. "I really shouldn't do this, but I need to. You see, I was an alcoholic for twenty years. Lilly saved me. She wouldn't approve. Now, who are you, really?"

Carter passed over his real credentials.

"United States government?"

"Yes. I must find Cory Howard."

She shook her head. "I have not seen Mr. Howard for a

very long time. I knew that he was a very dangerous man and that Lilly worked for him. Each time before she went away on business, she would call me. It was always the same. 'Rita,' she would say, 'I'm going away for a while. Take care of things.' That is what she told me this time."

"What 'things' were you supposed to take care of, Rita?"

The woman stood and disappeared into the bedroom. Carter couldn't be sure, but from the sounds she made he thought she was probably opening a wall safe. When she returned, she had a thick manila envelope in her hands.

"Lilly told me that if anything ever happened to her, I was to open this."

Carter waited tensely as she opened the envelope. From it she withdrew a thick sheaf of bills bound by two rubber bands, and a two-page letter. By the time she finished reading the letter, there were tears in her eyes.

She handed it over and stared down at the money in her lap.

Dearest Rita:

You are the only real friend I have in this world besides Cory Howard and my little sister. I know that when you read this you will do exactly as I ask.

Enclosed you will find $75,000. It is yours. I'm sure it will be enough to pay off your mortgage and take care of you for some time.

You will also find a key to my London flat. In the flat are all my financial records, bankbooks, stocks, bonds and such, as well as my will. I leave everything to my sister, Jova.

Please contact Arnold Kingsley here on Cayman and give him this key, as well as the Mayfair flat address which only you and Jova have.

Should anything happen to Mr. Kingsley, or should you not be able to get in touch with him, I want you to contact Cory Howard through MARCUS.

Good-bye, my friend.

It was signed *Lilly*.

Carter folded the pages and handed them back to the woman. "Who is Marcus?"

She shrugged. "He is some kind of an associate of Cory Howard's. All I have is a phone number that Lilly gave me a long time ago. She told me if I was ever in trouble and couldn't find her, I was supposed to call this Marcus. I've never had to."

She reeled off the number. Carter imprinted it on his brain and headed for the phone.

"Operator. May I help you?"

"Yes, Operator, I have a message to call a friend back. I wonder if you could tell me if it's a long-distance call." Carter rattled off the series of numbers.

It took only a few seconds and she was back. "That number is for Tortola, sir, in the British Virgin Islands. You can dial it direct."

"Thank you." He hung up and turned to Rita. "Do you have an atlas or a map that would have the Virgin Islands on it?"

She produced one from a nearby bookcase. Carter thumbed through it. Tortola was the largest of the mass of the British Virgin Islands. It lay just northeast of St. Thomas and St. John.

Carter retraced his steps to the phone and dialed.

"Tortola Bay Resort, may we help you?"

Carter hung up.

"Rita, tomorrow morning call Arnold Kingsley. Here's the number." He jotted it on a pad beside the phone. "Give him the key and tell him about the letter. But I would appreciate it if you wouldn't tell him about Marcus. All right?"

She nodded.

"I'm leaving now. If you want to reach me, I'm at the Tamarind. Also, it might be a good idea if you went over to Cayman Brac tomorrow and saw Jova."

"I will do it."

"And I doubt if it will be much consolation, but I've seen Lilly's will. Jova is a very rich woman."

He brushed his lips gently across the woman's cheek and left the bungalow. Retracing their steps through the garden, he entered the rear of the lounge. He was headed right on through, when the bartender called to him.

"Hey, man . . ." Carter stopped at the bar. "Good-lookin' little chickie-poo asking about you."

"Yeah? Know her?"

"Never seen her before. She come in while you were talkin' to Miss Rita, sat over there. When you went out back, she wiggles up and asks me if your name is Carter. I say, man, I don't know the dude's name."

"She leave a message?"

"Only the smell of a very strong perfume."

"Thanks."

Carter headed for the parking lot. Just short of his car he spotted a woman stepping from the shadows near the side of the building. He could see only the bottom part of her face—the lips—and they were smiling at him provoca-tively. Dark hair hung long and straight past her shoulders. A tip of tongue appeared at her lips as a hand came up, motioning him toward her.

"Sorry, honey," Carter growled, "I'm not in the market tonight."

He made another step toward his car and she spoke. "Cory Howard."

Carter swerved and headed in her direction. "What

about Cory Howard?"

"This way—I don't want to be seen." She was backing into the shadows, her jeans pulling tightly across a very flat stomach, her sensuous body curving toward him like an arched bow.

"Look, little girl, games I don't—"

The blow came from out of nowhere to land just behind his right ear. Carter lurched forward, only to be grabbed. There had to be two of them because his arms were twisted behind him from the left.

He tried to struggle, but the blow behind the ear had turned his arms and legs to water. He was in that gray area—foggy, but not all the way out.

"That tree!" a high voice said.

Carter could feel himself slipping further into blackness as he was half dragged, half carried several feet.

"I've got the handcuffs." It was the girl's voice, a British accent.

Suddenly he was slammed up against something solid. Then something was stuffed into his mouth and a rough-textured hood was pulled over his face.

"Carter . . . Nick Carter! I know you're awake!"

The Killmaster returned to consciousness groggily. Someone was slapping his head back and forth. As the fog cleared from his mind, he realized that he was attached to a tree. He could feel the rough bark against his hands and his wrists, as well as the handcuffs.

"I know you can hear me, Carter, and I want you to listen very carefully."

The voice. Except for the British accent, it reminded Carter of the old American actor, Andy Devine. It was raspy, hoarse, and it sounded as if it were coming from the depths of a well.

"Mr. Howard wants you to piss off," the growl continued. "You're only alive because you did Mr. Howard a favor or two in the past. But if you don't walk away from this and go home, Mr. Howard says he'll have to forget old friendships."

Carter felt a hand at his chest and something being slipped into his shirt pocket.

"That's the key to the handcuffs, Carter. Someone will find you. Remember, you keep trying to find Mr. Howard, you're fish bait. Good night."

The hard edge of a palm came down on the side of Carter's neck and he sank into a dark, bottomless pit.

SEVEN

As Carter fought upward from the pain and the blackness, he felt fresh air on his face and knew that the hood had been removed from his head. The next sense that returned was hearing.

"Wake up, man! You okay?"

Carter opened his eyes and slowly they focused on Sammy Davis, Jr.'s face. The gag was gone, but his throat was as dry as the Sahara.

"Nobody mugs nobody on Cayman, man," the young black exclaimed. "What is this shit?"

"Fraternity joke," Carter managed, and then coughed.

"Huh?"

"Nothing. Key . . . breast pocket."

"What key, man?"

"To the handcuffs," Carter said.

"Yeah?" His fingers fumbled in the pocket of Carter's breast pocket and came up with the key. "Yeah, cool."

As he moved around the tree, Carter's eyes finished their focusing. Standing a few feet away was the twenty-year-anniversary couple, she with her mouth gaping, he, white as a ghost with his protruding belly jiggling in fear.

"What's with them?" Carter asked.

"They heard you moanin', man, when they was leavin'. That old broad comes runnin' back into the joint screamin' you been killed. You loose now."

Carter rubbed his wrists and staggered away from the tree. "Thanks, folks," he said, and nodded to them.

"Was it a gang?" the woman asked in a piercing voice.

"No," Carter chuckled, "no gang, just a little misunderstanding . . . more a joke than anything else."

The couple backed away and practically ran to their car.

"Joke, shit, man—you got a knot on the back of your head like an egg. Should I call the coppers?"

"No," Carter said, feeling the lump and assessing the rest of the damage. "They wouldn't get 'em anyway." He peeled off a couple of large bills from the wad in his pocket. "Here, for your trouble, and your memory."

The little black shrugged. "Your poison, man. You wanna get beaned and laugh it off, it's up to you."

Carter clapped him on the shoulder and headed for his car. At the edge of the parking lot, something stopped him, held him.

He didn't put it above Howard to strong-arm someone to keep him off his back. But he would do it himself, not send someone else, even if they were pros. And the three who jumped Carter were definitely pros.

Another thing that grated on the Killmaster and didn't fit was, why? Howard knew him; they had worked together too many times. To toss a deal like this at Carter was like dangling raw meat in front of a hungry tiger, and Cory Howard would know it.

He reversed the car and pulled it out of sight into a grove of trees. Suddenly the trashing of Howard's house in Cornwall was a big item on his mind. It fit too well with tonight and the fact that he had just left Rita Lyon.

Outside the car, Carter staggered again, paused with his

head between his knees until the nausea passed, and then struck off through the garden.

The bungalow was dark. At the rear door, Carter dropped his hand to the knob and tested it. It turned and the door swung inward.

His jaw tensed as he moved into the room in a crouch. Even on crime-free Cayman, he suspected that people locked their doors before they went to bed. If Rita Lyon had been in the lounge she would have been drawn out when Carter was discovered handcuffed to a tree.

She wasn't, so she must still be in the bungalow.

Was she sitting in the dark?

Carter didn't think so.

He closed the door and flashed his penlight around the living room. Everything was just as neat as when he had left earlier. Even his empty beer bottle and her glass were gone.

The door leading to the bedroom and the one to the kitchen were closed. Carter called her name in a loud whisper. There was no reply.

He crossed the room in four quick strides and opened the bedroom door. In the light from the flash he saw her sprawled across the bed on her back, her eyes wide, staring vacantly. She was dressed just as she had been when he left her, only one side of the blouse had been ripped to her waist, exposing a bare breast.

There were dark, purplish bruises all around her neck. So ruthlessly had she been strangled that the finger marks could be seen by the naked eye.

Carter crossed to the window and pulled the drapes tightly closed. Only then did he turn on one of the bedside lamps.

There were only minimal signs of a struggle: a chair turned over, books scattered from the bedside stand, and her cosmetics swept from the top of the vanity table. The table was directly under the sofa, and it was gaping open.

It was fairly easy to reconstruct what had happened. They—or maybe just Gravel-Voice—had come in silently from the living room. Rita had been at the safe. The intruder had gotten her from behind. She had struggled. He had dragged her across to the bed, thrown her down, and then, with his superior strength, ended her life.

Quickly but thoroughly, Carter searched the room. Lilly's letter and the seventy-five thousand in cash were gone. On a molding ledge between the wall and the vanity he found the key to Lilly's London flat. It must have fallen from Rita's hand when she was grabbed.

Carter pocketed it and turned back to the bed.

He had seen it before, many, many times. But this one got to him. She had trusted him and he had led them right to her. This wasn't the gardener with the heart attack in Cornwall. This was cold-blooded murder.

As with physical pain, there is a merciful period of self-anesthesia that operates on the mind as well as the body to halt shock for a few moments.

It had worked for Carter the first few moments after coming through the door and seeing the lifeless woman. Now the shock as well as the disgust set in.

Now he knew.

Cory Howard was not responsible for this. They—whoever "they" were—were stalking Carter just as he was stalking Cory Howard.

Suddenly his teeth were clamped together so hard that his jaws began to ache. As he turned away from the bed, he realized that his nails were digging into his palms.

He placed one foot before the other and crossed the short distance to the telephone where it had been thrown from the vanity table to the floor.

He was the Killmaster again as he dialed, cold, as inhumanly aware and calculating as a machine. The phone rang and rang. Carter was about to slam it down in disgust, when Leona Kingsley answered.

"Hello?"

"This is Carter. Put your husband on, *now!*"

The exchange was so abrupt; Carter heard the phone clatter to the floor and the man's grunt as he bent to retrieve it.

"This is Kingsley."

"What have you got for me?" Carter waited a full five seconds for a reply, then hissed, "Dammit, *what?*"

"Nothing, I'm afraid."

"What the hell do you mean, 'nothing'?"

"I mean, Cory called me back just twenty minutes ago. I copied down what he said word for word so I could repeat it."

Carter sighed. "Okay, read."

"'Tell Nick to stay out of it. I've got to do it alone. If he gets involved, the bureaucracy is involved, and it's the damned bureaucratic power that started this mess in the first place. Tell him to mark it down as a loss and go chase the Russians. Thanks, but no thanks.' That's it."

"Shit. Just shit," Carter muttered. "The damned idiot. Listen, Kingsley, and listen good. You said Howard called you back?"

"That's right."

"Who did you call to get in touch with Howard?"

"Carter, I can't tell you that . . ."

"I could come over there and break your arms, one by one."

"Yes, I suppose you could." A raw edge had come into the man's voice. "I gave Cory my word."

"Do you know where he is?"

"That I can tell you truthfully. No, I don't . . . and I swear, Carter, that's the truth."

"Okay, I believe you. Did you make contact through another man?"

Silence.

"Good," Carter said. "Was that man's name Marcus?"

Silence.

"Even better, Kingsley. One last question. Does Cory Howard own a place called the Tortola Bay Resort?"

Not quite silence. Some heavy breathing.

"Don't worry about it, Arnie, old boy. Believe me, you're doing Howard a bigger favor than you realize. Now we get to the personal questions, and I want loud answers. Do you have any children?"

"No."

"Good, you can move faster. Do you have a boat?"

"Yes, that's why I moved to the islands."

"The closest port where you can get a plane out is Montego Bay, Jamaica. Will your boat make it that far?"

"Yes, easily. Look here, Carter, what are you driving at?"

"I might be driving at saving your life. I want you and your wife out of your house in minutes. And I mean don't close it up; just lock it up and leave. Get on that boat of yours and get to Montego Bay. From there, get a flight connection to London as soon as possible."

"London?"

Quickly, Carter gave him a synopsis of Lilly Kalensky's farewell letter to Rita Lyon, leaving out the part about Marcus.

"You're out of it now, Kingsley. It's the big leagues, with hardball and no more go-betweens. I'll get Jova to London to join you and your wife. Get rooms at one of the smaller hotels, like the Strand Palace. Do you know it?"

"Yes, but I never stay there."

"That's why you are now. I'll have Jova contact you there. You can pick up the key to Lilly's flat at London Central Post, General Delivery, in your name. There will be police, but you shouldn't have any problems since you have the key and you can identify yourself. Got it?"

"I've got it."

Carter could tell from the resignation in the man's voice that he was going to follow orders. "Good man, Kingsley. Now, one more thing. What's the number of the Cayman Brac villa?"

The lawyer reeled it off from memory and Carter nodded to himself. It was the same number Sharon Purdue had left for him to call earlier. Kingsley was playing ball, as much as his professional ethics would allow.

"*Ciao*, Kingsley. Move!"

He disconnected and dialed again. A sleep-filled female voice groaned, "Hello?"

"Jova?" Carter couldn't really tell who had answered.

"Yes."

"This is Nick Carter."

"Oh, Nick, it's so good to hear from you! Thanks for sending Sharon over. She's a lovely person. Will you be coming over? Will I see you?"

"Sooner than you think, honey. Listen, if I were coming in by seaplane, where would be a quiet, secluded place to land?"

"Let me think. . . . Oh, there's a cove around the western tip of the island from the Tiara Beach Hotel, about four miles. I think it's called Smuggler's Cove. There is a breakwater and the surf is always calm."

"I'll see you there in two hours. Put Sharon on."

"You're coming in the middle of the night?"

"Don't ask, honey, do! Put her on."

"Just a minute."

Carter thumbed a cigarette out and lit it, forcing himself not to look at the bed while he waited.

"Yes, Nick."

"Tell Jova to pack . . . light. She knows where I'll be meeting you in about two hours."

"Now?"

"Now. I'll gather your things from the hotel. I'm chartering a seaplane."

"Where are we going?"

Carter hesitated. "San Juan."

"Puerto Rico?"

"That's right." This time there was no hesitation.

"Howard?" she whispered.

"You got it. Two hours."

Carter carefully wiped the phone and everything else in the room he had touched. He turned out the light and made his way without being seen back to his car.

A half hour later he was gathering his and Sharon Purdue's bags together and descending to the lobby.

As casually as possible, he checked out.

"Hate to cut such a lovely stay short," he said to the desk clerk on duty, "but I've got urgent business back in Miami."

"I understand, sir, no problem."

"Thank God we came down on the yacht," Carter said. "Couldn't get a flight out this time of night."

"Your receipt, sir, your change, and the envelope and stamp you asked for."

"Thank you. Oh, I understand there's a restaurant, good Russian food, Borshov's, on the island. Thought I might pick up a snack to take with us."

The clerk checked his watch. "Eleven-thirty. Yes, sir, they will still be serving. It's over on North Sound near the beach."

"Thank you, thank you."

Carter addressed the envelope, sealed the key inside, and mailed it.

Eleven-thirty, he thought, walking toward the car. Ten to one, if he knew Arkady Svetov, the Russian would be at the Borshov bar sucking up vodka until closing time.

Carter parked directly across the street from Borshov's. He hadn't been followed to or from the hotel, and it hadn't been surprising. The hoarse-voiced man and his two companions had done their night's work. Carter wouldn't be surprised if they were already off the island.

Inside, it took a full minute for his eyes to adjust to the dim interior. He was about to head left toward the bar and inquire, when he spotted the Russian. He was sitting in a corner alone, with a half-empty bottle of vodka in front of him and a glass in his shaky hands.

A young waiter stood nearby in the inner doorway leading up to a stand-up bar. From his look, Carter could see that he was afraid of Arkady Svetov. At least he was afraid of what the man might do when the vodka bottle was empty.

"Bring me a brandy," Carter said, "I'm joining my friend there."

"Yes, sir," the young man gulped, and scurried away.

The Killmaster crossed the room to Svetov's table and sat down in a chair across from the Russian. There were a half-dozen stragglers nearby, most of them nodding as badly as the KGB man.

"Arkady."

He looked up, blinked, and glowered across the table with a red-eyed stare. Recognition was slow to come. When it did, he belched and smiled.

"Nicholas, you decided to join me at last."

"I'm afraid the dinner hour has come and gone, Arkady."

"Oh?" He studied his watch, gave up trying to decipher it, and refilled his glass. "Then it must be time to drink."

The waiter deposited a glass in front of Carter, gave the other man an anxious look, and hurried away.

Carter moved closer to the table, leaned forward, and lowered his voice. "Arkady, are you listening to me?"

"Of course. Only my mind is drunk. My ears are working perfectly."

"I need a favor."

"From me?" The glassy stare cleared a little. "What is it?"

"I need a seaplane and a pilot who doesn't ask questions."

Only half of his mouth smiled. "Ah, your holiday has been interrupted?"

"You might say that," Carter drawled. "I know you pop in and out of Cuba quietly every so often. How?"

"By plane, of course. How soon do you have to go?"

"An hour ago," Carter replied. "Price is no object."

The Russian sighed. "Ah, Nicholas, you Americans with your liberal capitalist budgets. Where to?"

"Cayman Brac, for starters. The next stop I'll figure out in the air."

The brows furrowed and a hot spark ignited in the depths of his red-rimmed eyes. "I do know of a pilot in constant need of funds. He has a sick mother in Caracas who gets sicker every time I talk to him."

"Help me this time, Arkady, and it will be like casting your bread upon the waters."

The old spy chuckled and lurched to his feet. "You know how it pays to gather favors in our business, Nicholas. I'll be right back."

He staggered across the room and into an alcove. Carter sipped his brandy and lit a cigarette. It was nearly five minutes before the Russian returned and sat heavily in his chair.

"His name is Luís Pedroza. The plane is tied up at Foreman's Pier on the north shore, not far from here."

Carter stood and dropped three twenties on the table. "Thanks, Arkady."

The Russian shrugged. "Call it my contribution to détente. Fly safe, Nicholas."

Carter made his way back to the car thinking that it was sad for spies to grow old. Without the satisfaction of getting killed on the job, they just faded away.

Carrying the bags, Carter approached a stucco shed with a hand-painted sign, LATINO FLYING SERVICE. Faint light showed beneath the door and through ratty curtains on the window.

He dropped the bags at the door and entered. A chest-high counter separated the office from the lounge area. The furniture was chrome, leatherette, and dusty. The wooden floor hadn't been swept in weeks. Behind the office, a burlap door led to the smell of fresh-brewed coffee.

"Anybody here?" Carter called.

The burlap parted and a stocky young man in blue coveralls with a white scarf knotted around his throat stepped through. He carried a steaming mug of coffee and chewed on an unlit cigar between even white teeth.

"Yeah?"

"Luís Pedroza?"

"Yeah."

"I'm—"

A hand came up, palm out. "You from Svetov?"

"Yes."

"Then I don't want to know who you are. You come recommended."

Carter shrugged. "I'll need you for three, maybe four days."

"Fine. I get a thousand a day and gas."

"Good enough," Carter said. "We pick up a couple of passengers on Cayman Brac."

"I carry anything or anybody anywhere. But I don't haul dope. I been busted twice already."

"No dope," Carter said. "You know Smuggler's Cove?"

"Like I know that rabbits fuck. Let's go."

He led the way outside, shutting off the light and pulling the door closed behind him.

"You don't lock up?"

Pedroza chuckled. "What for? Nothin' to steal. This way."

The plane was a single-engine Cessna with extra, long-range tanks bolted under both wings. Pedroza stored both bags and cast off the tie lines as Carter crawled aboard.

The plane's configuration was larger on the inside than it looked from the outside. The rearmost seat was fixed, wide enough for two comfortably seated passengers. The center seat had a split back to provide generous access to the rear by folding forward.

Pedroza slid into the left-hand seat and Carter took the copilot's bucket seat. There was a wide space between the two forward seats, which was filled at its lower level by a deck console and map compartment.

"Not exactly a stock model," Carter commented, and grinned.

"I don't carry stock cargo," Pedroza intoned, and hit the starter. The prop spun and coughed immediately. The engine roared loudly, and then purred contentedly when Pedroza retarded the throttle with an exaggerated two-finger movement.

He taxied the plane from the pier to the center of the bay

and turned into the wind. There, bouncing on the swells, with the engine idling constantly, he spoke. "Three or four days, you said?"

"That's right."

He held out his hand. "Half in front, cash."

Carter took a wad from a hidden pocket in his jacket and counted out fifteen hundred dollars.

"Nice doin' business with you, *amigo*. Hang on!"

He pocketed the money and revved the engine. With a quick look at the instruments, he wiggled the controls a final time and advanced the throttle.

The plane waddled through the swells and gained speed. They got off the water in a much shorter time than Carter expected, and the moment they did Pedroza eased back on the throttle and set the prop pitch for maximum climbing power.

"Smuggler's Cove is tricky at night."

"Can you set down?" Carter asked.

"Shit, man, I can do anything," the other man chortled. "That's why I get a thousand a day!"

He proved true to his word, banking the seaplane and gliding into the watery landing expertly and smoothly. He turned and stopped on a dime just a few feet from the beach.

The two women were waiting, Jova with a small bag in her hand. Carter shed his shoes and rolled up his trousers. One at a time, he carried them out to the plane.

Jova was quiet, her eyes wide with questions but staying silent. Sharon Purdue was full of questions. Carter silenced her with a look.

"Where to now, *amigo*?" Pedroza asked once the women were settled in the rear seat.

"San Juan," Carter said, leaning back and closing his eyes. "It's about a thousand air miles. Will your tanks make it?"

"They'll make it."

When they reached a cruising altitude, Sharon leaned forward to whisper in Carter's ear. "Have you really located Howard?"

"Yeah."

"When will you see him?"

"With any luck, tonight, after a good day's sleep."

Carter yawned and turned his head away before she could ask him where.

He was not about to tell her where he was going to meet Cory Howard.

EIGHT

It was minutes before dawn when Pedroza put down in the bay on the western side of the city. Customs met them at the pier. This proved no problem when Carter flashed a few papers and spoke the right names.

Pedroza helped him unload the baggage. "I think you'd be a great asset to my usual business, *amigo,*" the pilot said.

Carter chuckled. "Let's just say I've got a lot of clout with the right people."

"That you do. What's the plan?"

"Nothing for you until tonight," Carter said. "Do you know Point Puerca, on the west end of the island?"

"Yeah, there's a tie-up at the marina there."

"Be there at midnight tonight. I'll meet you. And when you leave, file a flight plan back to the Caymans. Can you handle that?"

"Need you ask?"

"Good man." Carter grabbed the three bags and joined the women at the end of the pier.

"What now?" Sharon asked.

"Taxi . . . hotel . . . sleep," Carter replied.

They found a sleepy-eyed cabby and drove to the Gran

Hotel El Convento in old San Juan. Carter checked them in and got a two-bedroom suite for himself and Sharon, an adjoining room for Jova.

"Grab a shower," he said to Sharon. "I'm going to let Jova in on her sister's occupation."

Alarm showed on Sharon's face. "You're not going to tell her what this is all about?"

"Of course not. We'll set up our own game plan for Cory when I get back."

He slipped down the hall and rapped on Jova's door. "Come in." She was sitting on the bed, looking for all the world like a sad, lost soul.

"Confused?" Carter asked gently.

"Very. But I trust you."

"Good."

He spent the next ten minutes explaining in as much detail as possible just what it was that Salvation Limited and Cory Howard did, as well as Lilly's part in it.

"My guess is they were trying to get somebody out, and in the process your sister was killed."

The girl took a deep breath and sighed with relief. "Then Cory didn't kill my sister?"

"No, quite the opposite. I think Lilly's death is what prompted whatever vendetta Cory has started. That's why I've got to stop him."

"Why have you brought me with you to San Juan?"

"Several reasons, Jova," he replied. "One of them is your safety, but I don't want to go into that now."

He had already tinkered with the idea of telling her about Rita Lyon's death and its implications, but scrubbed it. The girl was already confused and afraid enough as it was.

"Shall I go back to Washington?"

"Eventually, yes, but not yet. Arnold Kingsley and his

wife are in London. I want you to join them. Can you handle that?"

"Yes," she nodded, wiping her eyes and sliding from the bed.

To Carter's surprise, she threw her arms around him and pressed her body to his as hard as she could. Her perfume and the fresh scent of her hair filled his nostrils, and her strong, youthful body was doing strange things to his nerves.

Suddenly he realized that Jova was all grown up.

"At Heathrow," he said, his voice suddenly hoarse, "take a cab to the Strand Palace. Kingsley will already know what to do. Okay?"

"Yes," she said softly. "Nick . . ."

"Yeah?" He was finding it impossible to disengage her arms.

"Do me a favor?"

"I'll try."

"Stay with me tonight."

A volcanic ripple went up his spine. He looked down, only to find her lips coming up to meet his. The kiss was long and very sweet. But it was as full of loneliness and pain as it was passion.

"Maybe someday, Jova . . . but not now," he said quietly.

"I'm not a kid anymore, not now."

"Believe me, I know it," he said with a smile, "but I've got to take a rain check."

Finally he managed to extricate himself and move to the door, where he paused. "One more thing . . ."

"Yes?" She was turned away from him.

"After I talked to you and Sharon earlier tonight on Cayman Brac . . . did she make another call?"

Jova whirled, her eyebrows arched. "You and Sharon

don't get along, do you? I could sense in the plane . . ."

"Hey, slow down," Carter said, forcing a laugh to cover. "It's just a little interservice rivalry. Nothing to get excited about. Get some sleep."

"Nick . . . she did make a call. I didn't hear any of what she said, but I know it was long distance."

"Okay, see you in London. And, Jova . . . there's no need to say good-bye to Sharon. I'll do it for you."

"You really don't trust her, do you?"

"Let's just say I don't think she is completely what she seems to be."

He returned to the suite and his own room where he showered without an ounce of hot water. When he stepped from the shower he thought he might be awake enough to make the call he had to make, instead of hitting the sack.

He changed his mind when he stepped into the bedroom.

Sharon was lounging across his bed, her back against the headboard. She was wearing a blue negligee, an elaborate thing with built-in cups that pushed her breasts up and outward. The bodice was cut so low that, from above, Carter could look down and see a goodly quantity of soft, pale flesh.

"You mentioned something about a game plan?" she purred.

"Yeah," he said, tearing his eyes from her body and crossing to the mini-bar to build himself a nightcap. Or, in this case, a daycap. "Howard's here, or at least he will be, right after dark."

"Where?"

"It's an old sugar plantation on Topaz Road, about three miles outside Fajardo on the west end of the island. It's called Divino."

"That means heavenly."

"Yeah." Carter kept his face averted until he could erase his smile. When he was sure it was gone, he returned to the bed, drink in hand, and sat beside her.

"What time do we meet him?"

"I'll know what time *I* meet him after I make a call this afternoon."

"Why can't I go along?"

He shrugged. "Maybe you can. I'll know when I talk to Howard. In the meantime, I want you to rent us a car. Nothing showy, just transportation. We'll drive over to Fajardo and check into a hotel."

Silence fell between them. Carter sipped his drink and, out of the corner of his eye, caught Sharon watching him.

She looked a lot different at that moment. Her hair was down and tousled instead of perfectly coiffed. Her eyes had warmth, and the way she looked, with her lips partially open. . . .

Suddenly there was also something different about her beyond what he could see. It was a kind of electricity or tension, an excitement that seemed to crackle noiselessly around her. It was something that reached out from her and touched him.

"I guess after tomorrow it's over," she murmured. "You'll go back to Washington and I'll go back to a London desk."

"Depends," he said, finishing his drink.

"On what?"

"On what Howard's got to say. I think he's got a damned good reason for what he's doing. If he does, I might have to go back to England and have a long talk with Sir Charles Martin."

"Surely you don't think Sir Charles—"

"Sharon, right now I don't think anything. I'm sure you're as beat as I am, so why don't you trot on back to your own bed and let's get some sleep."

He snapped off the light, but found that the room was still fairly bright with daylight coming through the drapes.

When she didn't move from the bed, he tugged the towel from around his waist, dropped it to the floor, and settled into his pillow.

Then she was sliding down on the bed and her hands were working on the negligee. It disappeared, and through slitted eyes he took in all the delightful colors and curves about her.

Then her face was near his. He put his arms around her and pulled her easily against him. He opened his eyes wide then and watched her head tilt slowly to one side and her lips part. Slowly her lids dropped until her eyes were closed.

"Why, Miss Purdue, I do believe you want me to kiss you."

"More than that, you bastard. I plan on staying in this bed."

"That's all I needed to hear."

Her lips were full of fire with her body close against him, her perfume flooding his nostrils. She turned her face, rubbed her cheek against his. He pressed his lips against her throat and then her shoulder as he let his hands roam.

"You'd never know all this was there, with the clothes you usually wear," he chuckled.

"Must you talk?" Her voice was low and raspy now.

She undulated against his exploring palms, and he pressed his lips to her warm flesh. Her hands went behind his head to put it gently, pressing his mouth a little more firmly against her. Her fingers moved, the nails straying easily through his hair as he moved one hand against her back, holding her with the other. His hand traced the smoothly arching curve of her spine, caressed the mound that was her hip and her indented waist and then her breast.

She slid against him, her cheek touching his again and then her mouth against his, her lips moist, her tongue alive and restless, darting and probing. Her hand closed convulsively against his arm, the fingers gripping tightly and then relaxing, suddenly gripping again.

Her voice was hot in his ear, the breath washing against his neck as she said softly, "Nick, oh, Nick, darling. This is crazy. Darling, darling . . ."

It was too much, way too much, overdone. But Carter pushed the words from his mind. She wasn't reaching his mind now anyway.

The smell and touch of her reminded him of Jova's recent plea in her bedroom. But he pushed that from his mind as well, and concentrated on Sharon Purdue's ample, willing body.

Down, down he went, with his lips over her hard flat belly to her hip. She moaned and he bent to press his mouth against the softness of her other thigh. His lips were parted and his tongue savored her flesh. He moved his mouth up and down, teasing her.

Her belly undulated demandingly. "Oh, *please!*"

He kissed her all over, using verve and imagination, taking time.

Finally he pressed his lips against her crinkly, deep-set navel. She moaned sharply.

"Finish it!" she demanded.

He knew she didn't mean that. She was anxious, yes, but there was more to come.

He climbed onto his knees on the bed, between her legs, and fell forward on his elbows. He didn't enter her yet, but went instead to her high-surging breasts and lowered his open mouth toward one of the dollar-size beige circles that stared up at him, its sensitive flesh crinkled with tiny little bumps. The nipple at its center stood high and waiting. He kissed the aureole, pressing hard against the pillow of breast beneath it, and then he took the hard nipple between his tongue and upper lip.

She squirmed, moving her breast against his mouth, but he held the nipple fast. Then he brought his hands up to hold the large breast on each side and moved it back and forth as he relaxed his mouth and let the nipple slip around inside it and then bob out and back again. He did the same with her other breast until she was wild with desire. She was gasping and pulling at him, her legs flexing at his sides, but he still would not drive himself into the final phase of the act.

Instead, he leaned back on his haunches and said, "Turn over."

"Oh, Nick . . ."

She turned, presenting to him the small but pertly rounded cheeks of her bottom. When he lifted her hips at either side, she came up to her knees. He drew close, touched, and began teasing her. He supported his weight on her back and reached beneath her with his hands to shake and fondle her suspended breasts. The urgent rotation and backward thrusting of her hips caused her warmth to enclose him.

She moaned and he continued playing with her free-hanging breasts, taking both of them in his hand, squeezing them together, and brushing the very hard nipples with his fingertips. He moved his lower body only slightly, still teasing.

Suddenly she drew her legs up and turned around. As Carter sat back, she whirled, straddled his lap, and came down around him . . . all around him. She began jogging up and down, her breasts bouncing delightfully.

"Oh!" she cried. "Oh, yes, long and wild!"

He made it long and wild, bucking and driving, caressing her intimately with his fingers at the same time.

It was up, up, up into the breathless reaches of high passion until they extended themselves and seemed to touch the very stars. And then they plummeted downward and she hugged him and covered his face with openmouthed kisses.

"More," she murmured.

"You've got to be kidding . . ."

"More!"

For the next half hour they found pleasure after pleasure in each other's arms. No matter what it turned out to be she was involved in, Carter would always give her credit for knowing her way around a man's body. As an agent she was a wasted talent. Her true art was in bed. The surprise factor was one of her biggest assets in bed, he decided. She seemed to wing it, always doing what came naturally to her. Together they skirted ecstasy like two demons around the fires of hell before they finally went off on another fling into space and timelessness.

Sharon seemed determined to drive him to complete exhaustion. And she was almost succeeding.

"Tired?" she asked, when they finally lay limp in each other's arms.

"I'll say," Carter groaned. "Can't hold my eyes open."

"Let's rest a while," she purred, pulling away from him and fluttering the covers around him. "After all, we've got the whole long morning ahead of us."

Carter allowed her to arrange him on one side of the bed. He didn't open his eyes. And after a few minutes he adjusted his breathing to the long slow beat of sleeping. Another minute and he felt her move from the bed, heard her pad through the sitting room to her own bedroom. Through the two open doors he saw her dressing quickly.

Seconds later, she left the suite noiselessly.

Carter smiled himself to sleep.

The very slight click of the sitting room door awakened him. He barely cracked one eye. He could see her as she closed the door and turned the second lock. She moved into her own room and he watched her strip.

He took a quick glance at his wrist before shutting his eyes again.

It was one-thirty in the afternoon. Little Miss Purdue had evidently had a busy morning.

Carter continued to breathe the slow, relaxed way of a soundly sleeping person as she padded into the room and crawled back into the bed.

Then she was kissing him, gently shaking him. He fought her sleepily, and she lay quietly beside him in the dim light for a while before snuggling up to him again. This time she seemed determined to arouse him, so he allowed himself to be awakened.

"You've been sleeping a long time," she scolded, feigning a pout. It didn't become her. "It's after one."

"With you here beside me? Nonsense," he yawned, taking her into his arms but still acting out his drowsy role.

"Really you have, Nick," she insisted.

"Why didn't you wake me up?" he asked without opening his eyes.

"You were tired," she soothed, stroking his head with her fingers.

"Did you sleep well?" he said, his face shielded from her eyes by her own soft flesh.

"Like a baby." Her hand moved over his chest and abdomen in small circular motions he found more and more difficult to ignore. Then she raised herself up so that one hard-tipped breast bounced provocatively in his face, and he was awake. He opened his eyes and his mouth simultaneously, his hand reaching out to enclose the other breast.

"It's time you stopped ignoring me," she giggled with delight, and Carter truly admired her durability.

"Enough," he groaned suddenly. "I can't handle all these sudden personality changes on an empty stomach!"

He slid from the bed and pulled on his pants. While she combed her hair he ordered lunch from room service.

She was still playing the femme fatale when lunch for two arrived. Instead of hiding in the bedroom, she stayed on the balcony in full view of the young waiter with the sun shining through her negligee.

Over the food, she skillfully managed to get the conversation back to Howard.

"What will you do if Howard's story turns out to be true?"

"What story?"

"Why . . . I don't know. He seems to think he has something criminal on Sir Charles."

Carter kept his eyes on his food. "I'll probably talk to Sir Charles."

"But what if it's true?"

"Then I'll probably let Cory Howard go his own merry way."

Sharon gasped. "And kill Sir Charles?"

He looked at her sharply. "Do you have a better suggestion?"

"I . . . I guess I don't know."

Her face had paled and that stark, cold hardness had returned to her eyes. But it faded a little when Carter spoke again.

"I really enjoyed this morning."

"Thank you. So did I."

They finished the meal and Carter stood. "Gonna get dressed. Time to go to work."

They moved inside and parted in the center of the sitting room. Seconds later, in his own bedroom, Carter sensed her behind him.

He turned and smiled.

The negligee was a gossamer puddle at her feet.

"One more time?" she asked.

And Carter, with the premonition it might well be the last time he'd be with her alone, pulled her roughly into his arms. He was all caveman, no nibbling and coaxing and teasing, but all demanding and taking. It was as though he wanted to hurt her, but she writhed in pleasure, no matter how he bent her to his will.

NINE

It was three in the afternoon by the time Carter stepped from the cab in front of the slightly dilapidated old mansion. He was about eight miles from the center of San Juan, and he had taken two buses and three cabs to get there after buying a cheap suitcase and the items of clothing he would need for the coming night's work.

By now he could be fairly sure that no one was on his tail. But then, if his observations were in agreement with his calculations, they were probably figuring that there was no reason to follow him.

He gave the cabby—a jovial giant of a man with a tiny mustache and droopy eyes—an American fifty. "Will this make you wait?"

The man bit the bill, then cackled. "For this, señor, you can have my mother-in-law and you don't need Señora Pina's place!"

Carter laughed and, carrying the bag, moved up the wide steps under the stone portico. It was immediately ten degrees cooler out of the brilliant sun.

He rang the bell twice and waited. When nothing happened he rang again, several times. When there was still no response, he rapped hard with his knuckles.

At last the door swung open to reveal a sleepy-eyed

young girl blinking at the sudden light. She was stark naked, with small, erect breasts and blond hair, uncurled and falling to her shoulders.

"Oh, señor," she whined, "we are not open yet. We don't do business until six in the evening. Come back then."

She started to close the door. Carter caught it and stepped around her into the high-ceilinged hall.

"I'm not a customer," he said. "I'm a friend . . . of Señora Pina."

"*Madre de Dios!*" the young girl cried. "Don't tell her I answered the door like this. She will put me back on the street!"

Carter patted her cheek. "Your secret is safe with me. Where is she?"

"In the chapel," the girl replied, closing the door. "If you will let me get a robe, I will—"

"Never mind. I know the way."

Carter moved through the mansion toward the rear of the house. Little had changed in the three years since Señora Pina had hidden him in one of the many upstairs bedrooms and saved his life.

He walked through the spacious living room where nightly the girls met their clients. It had a massive stone fireplace, tall windows elaborately draped, and rich furnishings. The enormous rug on the floor was a genuine oriental, and the traditional furniture had been designed with a view to comfort as well as period style.

But then everything around Señora Pina had style . . . except, perhaps, some of her younger girls.

Through a small sitting room he entered another long hall. At the end of it there were three steps down to an ornately carved pair of doors. Carter opened one of them and slid into the dim chapel.

The only light in the windowless room came from tall tapers around the wall-to-wall, floor-to-ceiling altar.

As he slid quietly into one of the four pews, Carter could barely see the kneeling figure, all in black, before the altar.

The only sound was her whispered prayers.

He waited patiently, actually enjoying the quiet serenity of the room. He knew the woman was aware of his presence, but he also knew that nothing—not even a visit by the local police—could disrupt her morning, afternoon, and evening ritual.

Señora Pina might run the most exclusive and profitable whorehouse in the islands, but she was the most devout Catholic he had ever known.

At last, with a groan, the woman stood and walked up the aisle. There was no surprise when she saw him. "Hello, Nick," she said, kissing him lightly on both cheeks. "You are a long time away."

"Three years," he said, nodding.

"How is your wound?"

"Fine, thanks to you."

"No, thanks to God. He was looking over you." She smiled. "Come, we will have coffee in the sitting room."

In the hall she shed the heavy dark shawl from her head. Her jet-black hair had sprouted flecks of gray. It was pulled severely back from a pretty but worn, tired face. The figure, in an expensive black blouse and skirt, was still good, but the shoulders stooped slightly and Carter noticed that she favored her right leg.

They were scarcely seated when a maid appeared with a silver service and Señora Pina poured. It was as if he had been expected.

"What brings you back to San Juan?" she asked, handing him his coffee.

"The usual," he replied, accepting the fragile china cup and saucer. "Trouble."

"Ah, then you are still in the same line of business," she said, with a flash of even, white teeth in the still attractive, olive-toned face.

"I'm too young to die and too poor to retire," he joked with a grin.

They talked for another fifteen minutes about nothing and everything. Then she asked, "Well, what is it?"

"Does Santiago still work for you?"

"Of course." The smile faded. "Your business is not with him?"

"Oh, no, only that I need his help. I would like to have him in on this."

Señora Pina pressed a floor button with her foot and the maid appeared at once, as if she had been just outside the door.

"Sí, señora?"

"Where is Santiago?"

"I believe in the pool, Señora."

"Ask him to come in here at once."

"Sí, señora."

From the inside pocket of his jacket, Carter produced a map he had crudely drawn in the taxi. "Do you still own Divino?"

She laughed, a low, tinkling sound full of genuine mirth. "Of course I do. It's still my summer house away from the heat here in San Juan."

Carter matched her smile. He knew that the "heat" she referred to wasn't all weather. Every summer, for appearances' sake, the police would close her down for three weeks to a month. During that time, Señora Pina, Santiago, and her merry band of ladies would move shop to the big plantation house on Topaz Road outside of Fajardo.

Business, of course, wasn't as good from the coast and smaller city, but that was all right. They just treated it as a working vacation in the cooler mountain air.

"Is the old tunnel still there?"

She nodded. "Never used anymore, of course, since Chara died. But it's still there."

Chara had been Señora Pina's lifelong lover. He was a smuggler, and had built a tunnel from the plantation house to an abandoned schoolhouse nearly a mile away. Many times in the old days it had saved him from a jail sentence.

The door opened and Santiago entered. He recognized Carter at once and, like Señora Pina, showed no surprise.

Carter stood. "How are you, *amigo?*"

"Well, older, but still fit," the other man replied, shaking Carter's hand and taking a chair.

Santiago—it was the only name Carter had ever heard him called—was a tall man with thick brown, gray-flecked hair and a striking face. The lines were sharp, angular, strong. His features reminded Carter of a sculpture not quite finished, the head done in an ancient and rough Greek style, with the chisel marks and lines and gouges obvious in the stone.

When he sat he rested his hands, one over the other, on his lap. Like the man, the hands were large and strong.

Carter knew. He had seen those hands kill three men, quickly, quietly, efficiently.

"Santiago, I need your help, tonight and perhaps for a couple of days on another island. The pay is good."

The man swiveled his chiseled profile to his employer. She nodded and he turned back to Carter.

"What do I do?"

"I want to fool some people into thinking I am meeting someone at Divino. I will need five besides yourself. Can you get them?"

"The pay is good, you say?"

"It is."

"Then I can get all you want."

"Excellent." Carter smoothed out the map. "I don't know how many there will be, but I imagine they will already be on their way to Fajardo. That is, if I'm right."

"You mean," Señora Pina said, "this may come to nothing."

"Perhaps. I wish it would be nothing, but my instincts tell me they will be there." Carter turned back to the man. "And they will be good, very well trained. Your people will have to be invisible."

Santiago smiled. "They will be peasants from the mountains. No one sees peasants."

"All right. I want one man here at the fork outside of Fajardo. I don't know how many or how they will come up Topaz Road, but he will spot them."

"It will be no problem."

"Three more along the road spotting their progress, and a fifth man on the hill, here, behind the house to tell us what they do."

The big man's eyebrows furrowed. "I do not understand. What do you mean?"

"We want to be in the house." Carter laid the bag he had brought on its side and opened the lid. From it he took two identical white tropical suits and a denim jacket and bright yellow shirt. "I bought these this morning. You are about the size of the man they think I am going to meet. You will wear one of the white suits and this hat. Just after dark, I want you to drive out of Fajardo and meet me at Divino. I will wear the denim jacket and the yellow shirt. In the *casita*, I will strip and dress two dummies in my clothes and the white suit."

Carter knew that neither Señora Pina nor Santiago completely understood what he was driving at, but he also knew that they would follow his lead.

Santiago spoke. "Will we need hardware?"

"If you mean guns, no. We will need six high-powered walkies and a motorcycle. Can you handle that?"

Señora Pina stood. "I will make a phone call." She limped from the room, and Carter returned to the map, pointing to the rise behind the house.

"I want this man to be placed in such a way that he can see all approaches to the house and the interior of the great room."

"That is what you mean by 'observe'?"

"Yes. Have the bike ready at the schoolhouse. We'll ride to Point Puerca. I'll have a seaplane waiting for us there."

"It is a very elaborate plan to just 'observe.' If these men are your enemies, why don't we simply kill them?"

Carter's grin was clear across his face. "Because I won't know if they are my enemies unless they kill the dummies."

Outside, the last gray of dusk was just disappearing into darkness. Inside a small restaurant off the central square of Fajardo, a candle burned between them like a votive light.

The meal was finished. The check was paid. It would be only a few minutes until Carter would leave the restaurant, climb solo into the little Opel she had rented, and drive up into the mountains to Divino.

When he had returned to the hotel from Señora Pina's to tell Sharon that he would be meeting Howard at ten that evening, she had merely shrugged. When he had told her that Howard was definitely against seeing her, that he would meet only with Carter, she had shrugged again.

But beneath the calm exterior she was seething, and Carter could sense it.

"What is it . . . what's the matter?" he had pressed.

"When I came back with the car, I called Jova's room," she had replied between clenched teeth. "She wasn't there. When I inquired at the desk, they told me that she had checked out and taken the airport bus. Did you know about it?"

"Yes."

"I thought we were a team!" she exploded. "And, as half of this team, I think I should be informed of what's going on!"

Carter had plastered the most abashed, guilty look he could muster on his face. He apologized. He explained that it had been Jova's decision. He strengthened and compounded the lie by telling Sharon that Jova had no wish to stay in San Juan. And since he didn't feel she should go back to Cayman Brac, she might as well return to Washington.

After another five minutes of fanciful storytelling in his most contrite manner, Sharon seemed to accept that Carter's only real error was in not thinking the girl's departure important enough to raise Sharon's ire.

In the car, driving to the western end of the island and Fajardo, she warmed to him again. Now, sitting across the table from him, surrounded by the contented hum from other diners, she radiated the same warmth he had experienced earlier, in bed.

"You know, Nick," she said, "I really hope you can convince Cory to simply drop all this and come back to London with us and take it up directly with MI6."

"That would be nice," Carter agreed. "But knowing him as we both do, I doubt he'll take that route."

The thin waiter appeared, gesturing with his coffeepot. Carter raised his eyebrows to Sharon, who shook her head. The waiter moved on, slipping by the elbows of patrons like a matador avoiding the horns of the bull.

Carter stood. "When you finish your coffee, go back to the room. I'll phone you from up there as soon as I know anything."

Sharon nodded, tugging absently at the scarf knotted around her neck. "Be careful. You know Cory's temper."

"Yeah," Carter replied, and moved out of the restaurant with his mind trying to work through the façade of her face and find out how much real meaning had been in her last words.

Outside, walking toward the Opel, he tried to spot Santiago's man.

He couldn't. Other than a scant few tourists, everyone looked alike and paid him no attention at all.

In minutes he was outside the town and at the crossroads. Left went down to the ocean. In a few hours, Santiago would come from that direction. Carter turned right and started to climb. As he drove, he ran his hand under the seat and found the battery-powered walkie-talkie.

So far, so good, he thought. Santiago's people were on the ball.

He flipped on the power button and set the walkie in the seat beside him.

It was ten miles from the fork to the cutoff to Divino. Carter drove slowly, trying to spot the watchers. He couldn't, and smiled to himself.

About halfway up, the walkie crackled and a voice came through: "Señor C., this is Fajardo."

"Go ahead."

"The lady has left the restaurant. She walked to the center of the square and talked to a man on a bench."

"Could you get close enough to hear?" Carter asked.

"Not words, but the man had an accent—British."

The Killmaster had guessed right, but he didn't feel

good about it. The final tally on Sharon Purdue would come at the plantation house.

"She has left the man and is now walking across the square. I think she is going back to your hotel. Should I follow?"

"No, Fajardo, get on out to the crossroads."

"*Sí.*"

Carter waited a few minutes and depressed the "send" button again. "Let me know who is on the road."

A youthful voice came back at once in Spanish: "You passed me about ten minutes ago, señor."

And a second voice, older, lower: "You are just going by me now."

About three minutes later the third man checked in: "You are about three miles from me, Señor C. I can just make out your lights through the trees."

"All right," Carter said, "you all know the game. The minute they pass your checkpoint, get out. Your job is done."

There was a chorus of agreement and the walkie went dead.

Twenty minutes later he spotted the sign announcing the estate and passed through two tall stone arches. Two hundred yards of gravel drive wound under huge umbrella trees to the turnaround in front of the house.

Carter stopped and killed the engine.

The *casita* was part stucco, part brick, a rambling, two-story monstrosity built into the side of an emerald hill.

Carter picked up the walkie. "Anybody on the hill?"

"*Sí, señor.* My name is Manuel."

"How goes it?" Carter asked.

"I arrived just before sundown. I looked over the whole area. There is no advance man, señor, or I would have flushed him."

"Good. How's your view?"

"There is very little I cannot see . . . the drive, the front and rear patios, and both sides of the house."

"How about the bay window looking out over the rear patio and the pool?"

"I will be able to tell better when you are inside and there is a light, but it should not be a problem."

"Talk to you from inside," Carter growled, and got out of the car.

He took his regular small airline bag and the cheap suitcase he had purchased that morning from the trunk, closed it, and walked into the front patio.

A narrow walk was bordered by meticulously kept flowering shrubs. Señora Pina had told him that twice a week a gardener came up from Fajardo to maintain the place. The inside wall of the entranceway and the wall of the house itself were a mass of bougainvillaea vines with thousands of crimson and purple blossoms. Along the front of the house, dew-laden hibiscus clustered thickly on stocky bushes. A twenty-foot-high flowering poinsettia tree stood in one corner of the patio.

It was all very beautiful. Carter only hoped it looked the same way come morning.

He used the key Santiago had provided and slipped into the front hallway. By feel, he made it back to the great room overlooking the rear patio. When he had lit several candles, he slipped across the room to a large closet.

Manuel had done his work. Inside were two large male mannequins, their flesh tones a mahogany tan.

He carried both of them to the wicker table and chairs in the center of the room and opened the suitcase. When the larger of the two dummies was dressed in the white suit, shirt, and a string tie, he set it in one of the high-backed chairs facing away from the window.

Then he stripped, and dressed the second one in the dark trousers, yellow shirt, and denim jacket. This one he placed in a chair across from the first, so it could only be partially seen from through the window.

A final touch was a wide-brimmed Panama for the Santiago mannequin, and a fisherman's cap for his own.

It took him another ten minutes to kill all but two of the candles and arrange those two on the wicker table just so. When this was done, he opened the drapes and grabbed the walkie.

"Manuel?"

"Sí?"

"How does it look?"

After several seconds, the voice came back. "Very good, señor. If you could move the candle on your right just a little toward the window?"

Carter did. "How's that?"

"Perfect. I am looking through field glasses, and they are very lifelike."

Carter dressed, grabbed his flight bag, and made his way down to the wine cellar. With the aid of his penlight, he found the proper wine rack and pulled it inward. Behind it was a trapdoor with a large metal ring. He opened it and went down the dozen steps to the tunnel.

There he left his bag and a lighted candle. Leaving the trap open, he returned to the great room, where he built a drink at the bar, lit a cigarette, and sat back to wait.

"Señor C. . . ."

"Yes?"

"This is the halfway point. Santiago has just passed me."

"Good. Fajardo?"

"Nothing yet, señor. There has been no one approaching the crossroads since Santiago passed by."

"Stay alert," Carter said, and he did a last once-over of the room to make sure the scene was set.

"This is number three. Santiago is just opposite me."

"Check."

Carter moved to the front of the house. He unlocked the front door, left the key in the lock and the door ajar, and returned to the great room. Carefully, he arranged glasses half full of brandy and a bottle on the table. To these he added cups, saucers, and a carafe of steaming coffee.

As a last touch, he used his penknife to drill a hole in the Santiago dummy's mouth. From a box on the bar he got a cigar and lit it. When it was going steady and even, he inserted it and stood back.

"A touch of genius, if I do say so myself," he said to himself and chuckled.

"Señor C. . . ."

"Yes, Manuel?"

"Santiago has arrived."

"I hear him."

Moments later, Santiago lumbered into the room, carrying a small flight bag. He took everything in with one glance, and grinned. "A work of art."

"Thank you, *amigo*. Did you lock the front door?"

The man held up the key.

"Señor C., this is Fajardo."

"Yes?" Carter said.

"If it were a baseball game, you would have just hit a home run."

"How so?"

"Five men, one woman. They are in two cars. They just passed the crossroads and went up Topaz Road."

"Did you recognize the Englishman you saw earlier with the woman?"

"*Sí, señor*. He is driving the lead car. They are going very fast."

"All right, Fajardo, you get back to the hotel and keep track of the lady. We'll get a report in the morning."

"*Sí. Vaya con Dios.*"

Carter lowered the walkie. "Change."

By the time Santiago had changed into a dark turtleneck and black trousers, checkpoints one and two had announced the caravan's passing.

"They are moving fast," Santiago said.

"Yeah," Carter hissed, "they sure as hell are."

"Señor C.?"

"Yes."

"This is number three. They have pulled off the road just below me and left the cars. They are all armed . . . machine guns, I think. The men are moving on toward the house. The woman is staying behind. It looks like she is covering their rear down the road."

"Manuel," Carter said into the walkie, "did you get that?"

"*Sí.* I have two of them in my glasses. They have left the road and are coming up through the trees."

"Okay, Manuel, it's all yours."

"*Sí, señor.* I will memorize what faces I can see clearly."

"Santiago, let's go!"

The two men raced to the wine cellar. They pulled the wine rack flush behind them and secured the trapdoor. Carter found his bag, and Santiago led the way through the tunnel with a powerful flashlight.

Only twice did they hit water, so less than five minutes had elapsed before they were crawling through a second trapdoor opening into the moonlight.

"The motorcycle is there, in the woods, under a tarpaulin."

"Roll it out," Carter replied, and brought the walkie to his lips. "Manuel?"

"They are all around the house, señor. One man has climbed the palmetto tree and is going through a second-story window. Two are somewhere in the front courtyard, and the other two are going over the wall to the rear patio. Now those two—"

Suddenly Manuel's voice was drowned out by the chatter of gunfire. Even without the aid of the walkie Carter could hear it clearly through the hills.

It seemed to go on forever and then, just as suddenly as it had started, it stopped.

Carter waited a few seconds and spoke into the walkie. "Manuel?"

"Señor, if it had been you and Santiago in there, you would now have been with the angels. They are inside. Wait . . . they have discovered the trick. Three of them are going through the house . . . the other two are outside, searching."

"Sign off, Manuel, and watch yourself," Carter growled, and turned to Santiago.

"Have you observed enough?" the man asked.

"Yeah, I sure as hell have. Crank that thing up. Let's get the hell out of here!"

At midnight sharp, they turned the motorcycle over to one of Santiago's people at the Point Puerca marina and climbed into the plane.

"Santiago, Luís Pedroza," Carter said, opening a map.

The two men nodded and Pedroza looked down at the map. "Where to?"

"Tortola. Do you know someplace you can dump us so we don't have to go through customs?"

"Yeah, right here. There's a deep cove just west of Brewer's Bay. I can be down and gone before anybody knows we've even landed."

"Perfect," Carter said, handing the pilot an envelope. "There's a fat bonus in there for your trouble."

Pedroza pocketed the envelope and started the plane. "Like I say, *amigo*, it's a pleasure doin' business with you."

Five minutes later they were cruising high over the ocean.

TEN

The tall, suntanned girl behind the desk wore an off-the-shoulder, low-cut blouse that hid none of her physical attributes. She was also genuinely pretty, with warm brown eyes set far apart, a provocatively soft mouth, a pert nose, and flawless skin, all framed by loose, raven-black hair that tumbled about her bare shoulders.

"Good morning, sir," she said, managing to retain her commercial smile even after taking in Carter's bedraggled, unshaven appearance.

"Mornin', darlin'. MacSweeney, Colin MacSweeney. Got my reservation?" It was a sloppy Texas accent, but she wouldn't know the difference.

She began punching a computer, still throwing sidelong glances at his face and clothes.

"Been one hell of a night. Had plane trouble out of San Juan, had to land in St. Thomas and take the ferry from there. Slept on a hard bench most of the night. Hell of a night."

Actually, he and Santiago had spent most of the night sleeping on the beach, and the better part of the morning hoofing it to where they could find a taxi.

"I'm sorry about that. Here we are, Mr. MacSweeney

. . . a suite?" She said it with amazement on her face, until she saw the wad he produced from his jacket pocket.

"I'll just give ya two days in advance. How will that be, darlin'?"

"That will be fine, sir." Her voice was like syrup now, and her eyes told Carter that he was her kind of man. "Take this gentleman to bungalow nine."

A young bellboy took Carter's bag, but before he followed, Carter leaned over the counter.

"I don't mean to be forward, darlin', but with only two days, a man's got to hurry a bit. What time do you get off?"

The smile got wider. "Three."

"Drink by the pool?"

She shrugged and the front of the blouse did wonderful things. "I usually drop by the pool when I get off."

"I'll just bet you do, darlin'."

The bungalow was deluxe, consisting of a huge high-ceilinged living room, an even larger bedroom, and a terrace with a view of the entire resort.

Carter pressed a twenty into the bellboy's hand. "Thank you, son. Say, ol' Marcus wouldn't be around this morning, would he?"

"He usually is, sir, but lately he's been sailing every morning."

"That so? When does he get back . . . usually?"

A shrug. "Depends. Sometimes in the afternoon, sometimes not until evening."

"I see," Carter said, pressing another twenty in the boy's hand. "Well, if you see him, don't tell him I'm here, will ya? We're ol' friends and I want to surprise him. Okay?"

"Sure." He started for the door.

"Say, what kind of a boat is Marcus sailin' now?"

"It's the hotel's, a thirty-footer, two-masted, called the *Lilly.*"

It would be, Carter thought, and smiled the young man out before he dived for the island directory. He looked up the number where he had left Santiago off, and dialed.

"The Sea View, good morning."

"Mr. Santiago's room, please."

It was answered at once.

"It's me. Marcus takes a sail every morning on the hotel boat. It's called the *Lilly.* Ask around and see if you can find out where he goes. Also try to pick us up a boat."

"Any particular brand?"

"The *Lilly* is sails. Pick us up a fast inboard."

"Will do."

"I'm in bungalow nine. I'll be by the pool around three."

"I'll see you then."

Carter hung up and trailed clothes to the shower. When he had all the sand washed off, he shaved and returned to the phone. When he had the AXE message center machine in Washington, he delivered a cryptic location-giver.

"N3 to N1 as MacSweeney, Tortola Bay Resort, number nine," he said, and hung up.

As he spoke, he leafed through the "Things To Do" brochure for the resort. On the last page his eye fell on the masthead listing the staff.

At the very top was ALEXANDER MARCUS, MANAGER.

The Tortola Bay Resort was built on a finger of lush green jutting out from the island itself. The bungalows— about forty of them—ringed the end of the finger, with the large main building containing offices and rooms in the center. It was all stone, with lots of domes, arches, and filigree.

In fact, the whole setup looked as if it had been designed by an architect who'd read *Tales of the Arabian Nights* once too often.

At a quarter to three, Carter rolled off the bed where he had sprawled into instant sleep, and made for the bath. After splashing a lot of cold water on his face, he climbed into a pair of trunks, grabbed a towel, and headed outside to the pool.

He ordered a gin and tonic, designated a chaise with his towel, and dived in. The pool was like tepid bath water but still refreshing. After a dozen laps, he climbed out to find his drink waiting. He settled into the chaise, lit a cigarette, and glanced around.

At three-fifty a night for a room—and five hundred dollars and up for a suite or bungalow—the Tortola Bay Resort didn't attract Aunt Fannie and Uncle Jud from Dubuque. Nearly every face he saw he recognized from magazines or newspapers.

Two chaises away, an Italian actress was being overdramatic with a French Formula One driver while her producer husband, looking bored, half listened to a Hollywood starlet whose eyes and conversation reflected the previous night's tactical mistakes.

Just beyond them, a sleek New York model who had recently become disengaged from her husband—a Detroit motor executive—was bending the ear of a famous Spanish painter. The gist of the conversation seemed to be detailed instructions on how to paint his next masterpiece.

The painter seemed far more interested in the perfection of line and form poured into her plunging swimsuit.

The model looked up long enough to give Carter an aristocratic and tolerant smile, and quickly went back to her stream of atrocious Spanish.

Suddenly Carter noticed all the male heads around the

pool turning in his direction. Then a shadow fell across him and he looked up to see why.

"Hello."

"Hello, darlin', sit right down."

She oozed into the chaise beside Carter, and the Italian star and Hollywood starlet turned green.

They had every reason to. In her string bikini, the dark-haired desk clerk looked as good or better than any of the exotic, international beauties sunning themselves there.

"Sorry I'm late. I got a call from my boss. He won't be back until late. I'll have to do the five o'clock audit."

Carter perked up. "That would be ol' Marcus."

"You know Alex?"

"Well," Carter drawled, "let's just say I know his boss."

"His boss?" She looked perplexed, and then a little light came on in her eyes. "Oh, you mean Cayman International?"

"Yeah," Carter said, leaning close enough to absorb some of the ample heat from her body. "I'll let ya in on a little secret, darlin' . . ."

She leaned a little herself, until her lips were breathing on his. "Oh, I love secrets."

"Ya see, I own quite a chunk of Texas, but what with oil the way it is now, I'm lookin' to diversify."

"Really?" The light in her eyes had literally made them turn green, the color of money. If she appeared to be something of a dingaling, it was all an act. "For instance," she continued, "in the islands?"

"You might say that. 'Course, I wouldn't want it nosed around and make the price go up . . ."

"Of course not."

"This Cayman International is a little tight-mouthed about their assets, and like any good businessman, I like to know if they're keepin' a plum back when they're offerin' the apples."

She rolled to her side and faced Carter. The movement dislodged one breast from its tiny crocheted cup. If she noticed, she did nothing about it.

Carter guessed she noticed.

"Could I be of any help? I've been with the resort for three years and do most of the internal bookkeeping."

Oh, brother, Carter thought, *wait until I tell Howard about his loyal employees!*

"Darlin', those words are music to my ears," he replied, and then abruptly changed the subject. "By the way, where is Marcus?"

"I don't know. He called from the ship-to-shore phone on the boat."

"That so? When do ya reckon he'll be back?"

She shrugged. "Probably not until at least midnight. He asked me to check out the eleven o'clock turnover on the desk."

Carter nodded, his face a mask of deep concentration. "One of the bellboys told me Marcus has been doin' a hell of a lot of all-day sailin' lately. Wonder where he goes . . ."

The dark eyes narrowed and Carter sensed bells of caution going off in her pretty head. He saw Santiago approach one of the two pool bars and take a stool.

"But I guess if you're the manager, you can play whenever ya want to, can't ya. But, say, darlin', here we are jabberin' and my manners have gone to hell. What would you like to drink?"

"A gin and tonic, no lime," she replied, relaxing and regaining the smile.

"Be right back," he said, rising. "By the way, darlin', what's your handle?"

"Handle . . . ?" She flushed a little and rewrapped the errant breast. Carter could hear the audible groans from the nearby males.

"Your name, darlin'."

"Oh . . . Eugenie."

"Well, Genie honey, you just bake there for a minute and ol' Mac will be back with the refreshments."

Carter jogged around the pool and made the stool beside Santiago just before a plump matron who looked like the front window of Cartier's grabbed it.

"Couple of gin and tonics, pardner . . . make one of them a double." The barman moved away and Carter spoke, barely moving his lips and without turning his eyes or head toward Santiago. "Got anything?"

"A couple of fishermen have spotted him leaving the past three days. Evidently, one man sailing the *Lilly* is a rough case . . . that's why they noticed."

"Did they see his route?"

"Watched him cut into the channel between Great Camanoe and Scrub Island, then he disappeared. A charter captain told me he spotted Marcus heading past the Dogs . . . that's three small islands about four miles east of here."

"There must be thirty or forty uninhabited and privately owned islands in the Virgins," Carter growled. "We don't have nearly enough time to check half of them. Did you get a launch?"

"Yeah, seventeen-footer, inboard. She's got a three-fifty Chrysler marine, and will do sixty easy and quietly."

"Good man. Where?"

"A little marina at East End. It's called Jacob's, dock four."

"Okay, I want you to get some night glasses and two scuba rigs . . . tanks, everything."

"We going out?"

"Yeah. The little lady says Marcus won't be back until midnight or later. If I can narrow the islands down, we'll try to spot the *Lilly*."

"You're sure he's not on Tortola?" Santiago murmured.

"Pretty sure. If Marcus is making daily runs, it's probably to take Howard supplies and get instructions. That would mean no phone."

"Got you," Santiago replied. "What time?"

"I'll try to make it at nine. Be ready."

"Here you are, sir. The double has the bent straw."

"Thanks, pardner."

Carter signed the check and returned to the lounges.

"Here ya are, Genie darlin'." He handed her the double. "And may I make a little suggestion?"

"I'm always open to suggestions," she said, and smiled brightly.

"Well, it's only three-thirty, and it's gettin' awful hot out here. An' since you don't have to be at that desk until five, maybe we can avail ourselves of the air conditioning in my bungalow and talk about your place in the scheme of things when I expand Texas!"

Drink in hand, she was up and leading the way.

Carter had no more trouble following her meaning than he did her well-filled bikini around the pool. They came to the lawn surrounded by hedges, and she continued to take the lead to number nine.

She opened the door, took his hand in her long fingers, and pulled him inside. The door closed with a kick from her sandaled foot. Two soft arms closed around his neck. Glossy black hair streamed behind her as lush red lips lifted to his mouth, crushing against it. A darting tongue probed his mouth hungrily. She ground her hips on his, pressing her body against him, squeezing his neck so hard it hurt.

Finally she came up for air.

"You're my kind of man," she groaned hoarsely, and then the lips were back on his to smother any answer he might have wanted to make.

She was grinding again, then nipping, then biting. . . .

"What are you, a cannibal?" Carter panted at last.

"You're going to be the cannibal," she smiled, taking off. "Come on!"

The red message light was lit on the sitting room phone, but, for the moment, Carter ignored it. His mind was on other things.

Eugenie went through the sitting room like a young deer. It was obvious that she didn't have conversation on her mind.

By the time Carter hit the door, the top of the bikini was gone and she was working on the strings that held the bottom together.

When in Rome, Carter thought, peeling off his trunks and meeting her in the center of the room.

He tried to remain cool and maintain self-control, but he felt it melting away by the proximity of her bewitching, hot body, and the even hotter greediness of her lips.

Together they fell, side by side, to the bed. He plunged his lips into the valley between her breasts and pressed the soft mounds to his cheeks. They were firm and ripe, with the need for love almost screaming from their inviting nipples. There were two concentric circles in two shades of pink against the paleness of the skin where the bikini had shielded her from the sun.

"Oh, take me!" she hissed. "Take me!"

Carter began to kiss her shoulders, then the delicious mounds that stood straight up and seemed to tremble like two sand castles in a minor earthquake. And the earthquake was inside her, heaving her chest and making her hips writhe and her legs churn and sending little growls and moans from her throat. He kissed the nipples, felt her hands tear at his hair.

She tugged and urged until he was between her thighs. His hands slid under her writhing body to grip her as she found him with her own hands.

"There," she panted as she arched upward, enveloping him.

A momentary pause, and then violence. She wriggled beneath him and tossed her head on the pillow, clamping her long legs high around his back. She praised him gaspingly and in the most basic language, rotating upward at the same time, acting as if she could have taken much more of him.

He began a slow, methodical plunging.

"Oh, Mac," she breathed, "you're sooo good. Ohhhh, soooo gooood!"

They moved in perfect rhythm, lunging and rotating. Their bodies slapped and the bed groaned sharply. Carter felt himself ascending. Again, now that he was in the midst of it and taking her, he felt the sense of detachment, almost as if he were standing back and watching another couple perform the act.

The physical building of passion—slowly and evenly—didn't detract from this curious mental sensation. He propped himself on his arms and watched her lust-contorted features as she voraciously took all he had to give her. He quickened the pace of his thrusts. She gasped and groaned, demanding still more. He tried to match her, but her thrusts were too erratically swift, and so he merely held himself in place, slightly elevated, and let her do it all.

She cried out and shrieked, seeming to take him in a great opening surge that was hot and all-consuming. He hit her with a torrent of short, savage strokes, made it over, and began to recover. They both were still.

She cooed against his ear and petted his back and hair, and then she pulled his face around and kissed him with her mouth as hot and moist and open as a mouth can be.

She talked against his lips and tongue in incoherent gasps.

Well, he had done his duty, Carter said to himself, and it hadn't been bad, of course.

But now he forced his mind to take over from his body.

"Tell you what, darlin'. . ."

"Yes?"

She was doing things with her hand. It took all his will-power to ignore it. "What time do you finish at the desk?"

"About six."

"Well, why don't you pop over to your room and climb into something fancy. Then I'll pick you up in your office about six-thirty and we'll have an early dinner."

"And after dinner?" she whispered coyly.

"Why, darlin', need you ask? Now just scoot along. I got to call my bankers."

Reluctantly, she left the bed and dressed. "I could just meet you in the dining room . . ."

"No, no, can't do that, darlin'. I'm a gentleman. I'll pick you up!"

He waited until he was sure she was well gone before climbing into his trunks and hitting the pay phone between the bungalows.

Hawk wasn't in, but that didn't really matter. He got the big man's good right arm, Ginger Bateman, and she was up on the whole mission as if she were Hawk himself.

Carter brought her up to date on everything in sharp detail, and included the plan for the coming night's events.

"It sounds sticky and very, very shaky," she said when he paused for breath at last.

"I agree, but where we pin it I don't know, and I might not know after seeing Howard. I'd like to risk putting people on all three of them."

"Sir Charles, Avery, and Hutchins?"

"That's right," Carter replied. "Don't know what we

can find, but it's bound to be more than we've got."

"Since Hutchins is CIA, he should be no problem. The other two? . . . Hard to say, but I'm sure Hawk will go along."

"Use free-lance in England. You've got a list."

"What about Sharon Purdue? Sounds like she's in up to her earrings."

"No doubt about it. Her, too, if you can find her. Now, anything for me?"

"Are you sitting down?"

"No chair," Carter said, "but give it to me anyway."

"You've joined Howard's club."

"How so?"

"Remember your kickoff contact in London?"

"Otto Luderman, yeah."

"He's dead. Someone sliced him from ear to ear with the jagged edge of a broken bottle."

Carter felt an ice-cold chill ripple up his spine and raise the hairs on the back of his neck. "And my prints were all over the bottle."

"Bingo, superspy. And that ain't all."

"Rita Lyon," he said hoarsely.

"You get to open door number two. They are combing the islands for you, so you've only got so much time."

"Let's hope I use it wisely. Give my best to the man."

Carter hung up. As he jogged back to the bungalow, he found himself darting looks over his shoulder.

There was no doubt about it now. He and Cory Howard were being royally set up.

ELEVEN

Carter barged right past the young night clerk with the hail-fellow-well-met attitude he had already established, and entered Eugenie's office.

"Here I am, darlin', right on time!" He gave her lips a brushing kiss and got a radiant smile in return. The dress she wore told him she had decided to go all out in this seduction for a better position of employment; the black silk dipped and clung to her every ample curve.

"I'll be just a moment," she purred.

"You just take your time, Genie."

Carter perched on the edge of the desk where he could take in the whole of the office, and lit a cigarette.

It took her five minutes to finish up what she was doing. In that time Carter perused the white cards on the fronts of file drawers and every other labeled piece of information he could see.

By the time she was locking up with a small ring of keys, Carter had spotted the file drawer he wanted. It contained the tax returns for the last seven years.

"Ready," she said, holding the door.

"Then let's do it!"

She locked the door, and arm in arm they entered the dining room.

It fit the rest of the resort perfectly, with low-key lighting and high prices. A velvet rope was stretched before the three steps leading down to the main room. A headwaiter in a tuxedo practically leaped at it when they appeared, bringing a smile to Carter's face.

Little Eugenie had spread the word about the investment baron from Texas.

They were shown to one of the very private booths near the dance floor. Carter ordered drinks, dinner, and wine all at the same time, bringing a lifted eyebrow from the woman.

"No matter how good the food is, darlin'," he countered, "we don't want to waste the evening eating, do we?"

She laughed and swayed against him, clutching his arm and letting him feel the pneumatic surge of her breast. "You make me feel like Cinderella!"

"How sweet. Drink up." He signaled the waiter for two more doubles.

From the salad through the entree he kept up a steady patter that kept her mind off the fact that she was drinking as much or more than she was eating.

Over dessert, Carter disdained coffee and ordered brandy instead.

They had been seated a minute or two after seven. At 8:05 he signed the check, rose, and reached for her hand. She never realized that she had been so whisked through a dinner.

He held her up all the way back to bungalow nine. By the time they got inside she was walking on the sides of her shoes instead of the heels.

The moment they were in the door, Carter got amorous. His hands worked at her hips, tugging her close.

"Ohhh, what a *tiger!*" Her voice dipped low on the last word and roughened sexily. She tried to say more, but gave up when her tongue got twisted up in her teeth. Instead, she tried to drill two holes through his chest with her breasts.

"Why don't you run into the bedroom and get sexy, darlin', while I fix us a little nightcap?"

"Oh, I don't know if I can handle—"

"Sure you can."

She staggered away and the Killmaster hit the wet bar. He poured himself a glass of water, then swallowed a capsule recently developed by the AXE medicos that worked wonders to quickly neutralize the effects of too much booze inbibed in a hurry.

Two minutes later he walked into the bedroom, a glass in each hand. "Here we are!"

She had managed to get her dress off and that was all. At that point she had collapsed across the bed.

Carter discarded the glasses and efficiently divested her of the rest of her clothing. When she was naked, he slipped her body under the sheet and returned to the sitting room.

There were two sets of keys in her purse. He pocketed both of them and slipped from the bungalow.

Minutes later he was using a jimmy to open the rear French doors of Eugenie's office. Using a penlight, he went directly to the file drawer he had spotted earlier.

The third key he tried opened the drawer. Quickly he fingered through the folders until he located the corporate tax return for the previous year.

He found what he wanted on page twenty of the return: property taxes paid on two islands called Big Rock and Little Rock.

He replaced the folder and locked the drawer. On a wall map he traced the route that Santiago's fishermen had given for Marcus and the *Lilly:* around Scrub Island and on to the Dogs. If Marcus had proceeded on east and slightly north, he would have hit the tiny Rock Islands.

Carter was willing to bet a month's pay that he had his route.

There were three keys on Eugenie's second ring. One was to room 419 in the hotel. The other two belonged to a Ford, and there was a small tag with the license number on the ring.

It took ten minutes of prowling the parking lot before he found a gray Mustang that matched the tag.

He hit the East End section with five minutes to spare before nine o'clock.

When the car was parked and locked, Carter hurried down the promenade that ran along the piers of the marina. There was very little sound except the lapping of the water and music from a hotel up the beach. Somewhere to his left, probably on a boat, a woman began to laugh. The laughter was strident and breathy, as though she were being tickled.

Then he spotted the right number. Ten steps out onto the pier, Santiago appeared like a specter out of the darkness.

"This way!"

The boat was low in the water, fast and sleek, perfect for their needs. From a console between the two bucket seats, Santiago produced a nautical map of the islands.

"Here," Carter said. "They're called Big Rock and Little Rock."

The engine roared to life, and seconds later they were lurching through the opening in the stone breakwater toward the open sea.

"There," Carter called, "through those bending trees, a cove!"

It was impossible in the darkness to see any shape with the naked eye. But with the night glasses, one of the masts and a portion of the *Lilly*'s gleaming white side was distinguishable.

"He's making sail," Santiago said, handing Carter the glasses.

The Killmaster refocused for his own eyes and trained the glasses. He saw a single man on the aft deck, and then the *Lilly* was moving.

"He's coming out," Carter hissed. "Over you go."

Both men had already donned the wet suits, masks, and flippers. Santiago had strapped one of the small-tank scuba rigs onto his back. The words were scarcely out of Carter's mouth when the man rolled over the side and quickly disappeared.

Carter let the launch idle him further around the island. When the *Lilly*, already out of the cove, was out of sight, he upped the throttle just enough to give him about five knots, and entered the fairly wide channel between the two islands.

When he figured he was just opposite where the *Lilly* had been moored on the other side of Big Rock, he killed the engine and dropped anchor.

Then, standing up in the boat, not giving a damn about his silhouette against the moonless gray night sky, he slipped into the scuba tank. When it was secure and the air mixture was right, he slipped into the crystal-clear water.

It was about two hundred yards to the sandy beach. He came up only once for bearings. His feet hit bottom twenty yards out and he kicked off the flippers. When the water was just below his knees, he dashed for the thick undergrowth and trees. Once there, he shed the tank and took a bearing off the bobbing boat behind him. Shod with sneakers he had attached to his utility belt, he struck off inland.

The island was like a one-humped camel with the spine

running the long way. It was hard going uphill, and then, over the hump, hard to keep a slow pace going down the other side.

He could see the ocean again when, about halfway down, the thick foliage began to thin out. Moments later he spotted a clearing to his left and veered that way.

Then he saw it, shrouded by the trees: a small, one-story stucco job with an honest-to-god tin roof. Smoke belched from a stovepipe at one end, and a water tank had been erected at the other. There wasn't a sign of an electric wire or a telephone line.

Primitive living at its best, Carter thought, but one hell of a place to hide.

From where he stood, a path led directly down to the house. Without worrying about noise, he started down. He was counting on the fact that Cory Howard already knew he was there, so the man wouldn't shoot his visitor without identifying him first.

Carter left the path when it petered out at the narrow clearing around the house. He was just approaching the front door, when a flash came on behind him, fully outlining him in its glare.

"Keep the hands where they can be seen, no quick moves. Turn around very slowly."

Carter did. "Hello, Cory."

"Hello, Nick. I thought it was you."

"It's been a long hunt, Cory," the Killmaster said, barely making out the Walther held steady in the man's hand. "Not thinking of shooting me after I've worked so hard, are you?"

"I don't shoot old friends, Nick. You know that."

"Then let's talk."

"Afraid not. I'm leaving soon. I'm afraid you've come for nothing. Inside."

"I may be able to help."

"Don't think so. You're loose, Nick, but you've still got to battle bureaucratic red tape. I don't."

"Cory . . ." Carter took a step forward.

"Don't do it, Nick. I won't kill you, but I'll put a slug where it hurts. Inside."

Carter turned and walked to the door. It was an old-fashioned latch. He lifted it and walked into the single large room. He could tell Howard had followed him by the degree of light. In the center of the room he turned.

"There's a hurricane lamp, there, to your right," Howard said, dancing his beam that way.

Suddenly a shape materialized from the darkness behind Howard against the wall. It moved quickly, without a sound. One arm went around Howard's neck, lifting him. The other knocked his gun hand down with a savage chop. The Walther clattered to the wooden floor.

Cory Howard struggled, but the arm at his neck and the knee in his back held him like a vise.

"His name is Santiago, Cory. You and I are good, but when it comes to a backup and night fighting, he's the best."

"Jesus . . ."

"Care to talk now, Cory? I'm in this as deep as you are, and I want out."

The big man sighed deeply and nodded. "Oh, what the hell. Let's talk."

Carter lit the hurricane lamp.

"So," Carter said at last, after an hour of hearing Cory Howard out, "your initial reaction was that you were double-crossed and fingered?"

Howard nodded. "That's it. I mean, they obviously wanted Marcel Longchamp dead. I jumped to the conclusion that the head of StarFire, Denis Jeansoulin, had fingered us. Hell, he was the only one I called to pick Longchamp up."

"But when Jeansoulin blew his brains out, you changed your mind and started digging."

"Right," Howard replied. "And it took a lot of digging, right on through about seven holding companies, until I found out that the principal ownership of StarFire went to Sir Charles Martin. Then, when Jeansoulin's secretary was appointed interim president of the company, I knew who had really fingered Lilly and me."

"Still a little thin to go after a fish as big as Sir Charles," Carter said, pouring them both fresh brandies.

"True, but Lilly gave me another solid clue before she died. The night I took her and Jova out, we had an MI6 contact in Subotica, Yugoslavia. He debriefed me and interviewed Lilly before he arranged transport for us to London. His name was Wolf Longbone. Many moons ago, Wolf caught a knife in the throat in West Berlin. He healed, but it left him with a strange, very hoarse way of speaking. It's like he can't get enough air to get his words out. Lilly swore to me it was Longbone who ran the raid the night she and Longchamp bought it."

Carter stayed calm. There would be time enough to inform Howard that it was ten to one Wolf Longbone was Rita Lyon's killer. "Go on."

"Do you remember my old secretary at MI6, Caroline Minor?"

Carter shook his head. "I never met her."

"Well, when I left, she was assigned to Sir Phillip Avery. After a year or so, she was shoved into the tunnel."

"Records?" Carter asked.

"Yeah. I contacted her a few days ago. She's on my side, and one reason is, she thinks Avery is playing some pretty weird games with MI6 economic intelligence."

"Like passing it on to someone who could profit highly from it?"

"Exactly," Howard said, nodding. "Everything I've found points to Sir Charles, but it's bloody hard to prove. The man is so insulated with wealth and layers of legal shelters, he's practically impossible to pin anything on."

"So you decided to draw him out into the open with an extortion bit. Not smart, Cory."

Howard smiled, almost a leer. "Oh? You're here, aren't you?"

"Touché," Carter said. "More on that later. What about Caroline Minor and this Longbone character?"

"When Wolf Longbone left the agency, he started a private security company, Protec Limited. They operate out of London, and they specialize in corporations operating in Third-World countries. Once again it took a lot of digging, but I found out that Protec is owned by a large holding company in Geneva."

"And that holding company," Carter finished, "is controlled by Sir Charles Martin."

"Bingo. I also discovered that, wherever Protec operated, a lot of important people died or disappeared. A lot of companies, like StarFire, suddenly came under Sir Charles's Geneva corporations."

Carter stood and began to pace. "So it would appear that the glue, or proof, if we can get it, is Wolf Longbone."

"Right. I had Caroline dig up everything in the MI6 records that Longbone had anything to do with or even had his name on. Right away she came up with an interesting little item. Longbone, even retired from the agency, still had total access to Records."

Carter froze. "That's a hell of a breach of security."

"And more. His authorization came from Sir Phillip

Avery. I asked Caroline to feed everything about Longbone into a computer and try to come up with a pattern. I got word tonight that she has come up with something that might be the key. That's why I was leaving for London."

Carter sighed and slumped back into the chair. "That's not going to be easy."

"I know, but I've come too far to stop now."

"Granted. What about those two international detectives, Guido Narboni and Jules Lafaye?"

"They're scum, anything for a buck."

"Did you kill them in Paris?"

Howard nodded. "Had to. I can't prove it, but I'd bet anything Longbone sent them after me. I was getting too close to Henri Liard."

Here Carter leaned forward until their faces were only inches apart. He told Howard in detail about Otto Luderman and Rita Lyon.

"Dammit!" the other man gasped, slamming the fist of one hand into the palm of the other. "That proves it. Everyone who helped lead you to me was whiffed right after you got the lead. That's it, Nick—once you reached me they were to waste the both of us!" Suddenly Howard's face lost a couple of shades of color. "Are you sure you didn't lead them here?"

"Positive. I figured out who was feeding them my movements."

"I'm listening."

"Our man Hutchins in CIA is thick as thieves with Avery. Only the two of them handled Sir Charles's intelligence. When I was given this mission, I was to contact no one else, none of our people nor MI6. They also saddled me with an agent from Sir Phillip's office. Tell me, Cory, what you can about Sharon Purdue."

What color was left in Cory Howard's face drained

away and he slumped further into the chair. "Oh, no. She was assigned to help you hunt for me?"

"That's right. Seems she was *very* close to you at one time."

Now the grin returned, lopsided and sardonic. "Righto, that she was. Sharon is a very ambitious woman. She is also the most nationalistic person I've ever known."

"How so?"

"All for Queen and Country, no matter what. If she had her way, Nick, the empire would have never folded. What's more, she would wipe out a third of the world to get the empire back. She's got tunnel vision—anything that's good for England is good for the world."

"That's a dangerous person," Carter growled. "The kind who sees a Communist under every rock and shoots before asking questions."

"That's Sharon."

"But would you say she is honest?"

"Oh, yes," Howard said, "she's blind, but she's honest. Sir Phillip Avery is just like her. If he told her to blow up Whitehall because of Communist infiltration, she would do it because she would think it was right."

Carter leaned back and lit a fresh cigarette. "That answers a lot of questions."

The Killmaster fell into a mood of intense concentration. Cory Howard saw and recognized the mood. He could almost hear the wheels turning in Carter's mind, and kept his silence.

And turning they were.

Sir Charles, Sir Phillip, and John Hutchins had formed a little intelligence triumvirate: you pat our back, we'll pat yours. Was it all for personal gain, or were they all doing what they were doing for their respective nations?

And what was the key that held them together?

Mines . . . mining . . . metals . . . precious industrial metals . . .

That had to be it, Carter thought.

"Cory," he said at last, "we're getting out of here. I'll see your Caroline Minor in England. I want you to try again for this Henri Liard in Paris. But first I want you to send another extortion threat to Sir Charles. Tell him that you are narrowing in, that you are extending the deadline. I'll inform Hutchins in Washington that I've missed you but I'm still close. I'll say I've tracked you to Rio or somewhere in South America. That should throw them off for a bit."

"You'll only have a few hours in London," Howard replied cryptically. "That's home ground for Longbone. He'll have the city covered like the proverbial blanket."

"I know. I'll just have to use every minute the best I can."

"Nick . . ."

"Yeah?"

"I think we're coming to the same conclusions. What if Sir Charles is using Avery and Hutchins to build his own empire?"

"It could be that Avery and Hutchins are using Sir Charles to feather their own nests and further their own philosophies."

Howard sighed and stood. "Or both."

"Or both," Carter agreed.

"What then? What if we don't get enough proof to push it all upstairs?"

"Then," Carter said, "I turn you loose."

TWELVE

The next twenty-four hours would be a sleepless nightmare.

Using the launch, Santiago ferried them back to the isolated west end of Tortola, where Luís Pedroza was still hanging around in hopes of picking up cargo, human or otherwise.

"Santo Domingo? Hell, yes."

Price was settled, and Carter penned a note to Eugenie begging her forgiveness for stealing off in the dead of night: emergency business in the form of a new oil find in one of his Texas fields.

Santiago would return the launch, her car, and plant a note in bungalow nine. He would also gather Carter's things and place the bag under the name of MacSweeney on a London flight. Then he would present another note to Alex Marcus penned by Howard. Marcus would see that Santiago got back to San Juan.

They hit Santo Domingo in the Dominican Republic around nine in the morning, just in time to catch a flight to New York.

"What makes you think they won't be watching Kennedy?" Howard asked.

"I don't," Carter growled, "but these marbles are all in England now, since they don't know if I made contact with you or not. My guess is they'll watch Heathrow and Gatwick."

That night they boarded the Concorde for Paris, where they split up, Howard to run down Henri Liard and put him on the griddle, Carter by train to the NATO airbase outside Brussels.

It was a long, roundabout, and time-consuming route, but Carter felt it would give him a few precious hours in London before he was spotted.

At first, General Mark Seever, head of NATO air command in Brussels, wasn't too happy about putting a jet at Carter's disposal. A phone call to Hawk and then the Pentagon changed his mind.

Two hours later, Carter landed at the military section of Birmingham's Midlands Airport wearing the uniform and double bars of a captain in the U.S.A.F. He taxied off the base and changed into workingman's clothing in the Brit-Rail men's loo.

The wait for a train into Victoria Station was less than an hour. Carter slept all the way, and left the train to immediately be swallowed up in the rush-hour crowd.

Wearily he moved around the huge structure several times before coming to a halt at the airport transfer area. He waited while a man with a flat Midland's accent claimed three bags, and then stepped forward and gave the woman behind the counter his identification.

"MacSweeney, Colin MacSweeney. I had a bag forwarded here from Heathrow."

"One moment, sir." It seemed an eternity, but at last she returned. "There you are, sir. That'll be four pounds twenty."

Carter paid her and hit the street. He passed several taxi

stands and made his way up Lower Belgrave. At Eaton Place, he flagged a cab.

"Hotel Bristol, Berkeley Street near the square. You know it?"

"Righto, guv."

At Hyde Park Corner they drew abreast of a police radio car. The officer at the wheel had his uniform cap tipped back and he looked bored. Carter wondered if Interpol had his picture out. If they did, that meant he had to dodge bobbies as well as Longbone's hordes.

He slouched further down in the seat.

"'Ere ya are, sir."

Carter paid and took his time walking across the street to the hotel. Through the first set of double doors he waited until the cab had driven off. When it was out of sight he returned to the street, zigzagging his way east to Old Bond Street where he hailed a second cab.

"British Museum, please."

They moved and Carter scanned other cars. Past the Ritz, the cab slowed in the crawling confusion of Piccadilly Circus. The driver was good. He maneuvered through the smaller streets and even managed to avoid the congestion near Haymarket.

From there it was clear sailing.

"You can let me off here."

The driver nodded without turning his head and reached back with a gnarled hand. Carter paid and jumped from the cab, just avoiding a bus on his way to the curb.

He skirted the museum, and when he was sure there was no one behind him, darted into Bloomsbury Way. The Avondale was in the middle of the block.

Carter checked in, using the third set of documents he carried, under the name of Field.

In the room, he dropped the bag and headed for the

bath. Stripped, he took the cold needles of the shower with gratitude, rubbing the weariness from his eyes and temples. Once he had shaved he felt alive again. Again he dressed in the plain brown tweed and rather shabby jacket.

There were two small airline bottles of Pinch in the bag. He popped one of these and sat down with the phone directory.

The closest television repair shop was in Russell Square, about ten blocks away.

"Universal Telly."

"Do you make service calls?"

"Yes, sir, we do. Mileage beyond two miles."

"Excellent. And how late are you open?"

"Nine this evening, sir."

"Thank you, I'll ring you back." He flipped the directory until he found the number of the Strand Palace. "Miss Jova Kalen's room, please."

He let it ring ten times and was about to hang up, when Jova's breathless voice answered.

"Jova, this is Nick Carter."

"Nick, I'm so glad to hear from you! Are you in London?"

"Yes, but I don't want anyone to know it. Do you understand?"

"Of course."

"How are things?"

"Fine. Arnold and his wife have been super. We're almost finished with all the paperwork. Did you know I'm rich?"

"Yes."

"I'd rather have Lilly back."

"I know, Jova. Just enjoy the money . . . Lilly would have wanted you to. I want you to do me a favor."

"Anything."

"Jot down this number: 441-579."

"Got it."

"I want you to call that number. A woman will answer. Identify her as Caroline Minor. When you do, tell her that her package at Christobel's is ready and ask her if she would like to have it sent around. Have you got that?"

"Yes," Jova replied, repeating it.

"Good. I want you to call me back at 949-771 and tell me what she says. Okay?"

"Will do."

Carter hung up and picked up his drink. By the time he had finished it, the phone rang.

"Yes?"

"It's me, Nick. I just talked to her."

"And?"

"She said that that would be fine. She'll be in the flat all evening."

"Terrific. See you soon."

Carter hung up without allowing a reply and left the hotel. Staying with his maximum security ritual, he took a full twenty minutes to cover the ten blocks to Russell Square.

Number 18 was just off the square in a tiny, alleylike street. It was a five-story building with yellow bricks and ugly stained glass in the first-floor windows. An old van was parked in front. Lettered on its side was UNIVERSAL TELEVISION.

But where was Universal Television?

Carter mounted the single step and lifted the door knocker. It opened at once, as if the woman had been hiding behind it. She was gray-haired, flat-chested, fifty, and she wore a mustard-colored dress three sizes too large for her.

"Yeah, wha' is 't?"

"Universal Television?"

"He's me ol' man, got his shop in the basement aroun' the side." The door slammed in Carter's face.

He walked around the side and down into an even narrower alley. The sign could barely be deciphered through the dirt on the glass. It said: UNIVERSAL TELEVISION, MONTE BABCOCK, EST. 1960.

Carter entered. "Anyone here?"

"In the back!"

He wound his way through the piles of old TV sets, cables, antennas and tubes to a smaller room. He found a large round man in blue coveralls sitting at a workbench.

"Mr. Babcock?"

The man turned on his stool and stared at Carter with eyes that appeared abnormally large behind thick metal-framed glasses. "Yeah?"

There was something about the man and the shop that told Carter he need look no further. "What's your normal charge for a service call, Mr. Babcock?"

"Twenty pounds plus parts."

"How would you like to make three hundred pounds for two hours' work?"

The moment Babcock pulled the van into the narrow street Carter spotted them. There were two of them, slouching in the front seat of a Jaguar sedan.

"Here," Carter said, and the van halted.

It was barely stopped when Carter jogged up the stoop and ran his eye down the mailboxes. Caroline Minor was in 5B. There was an L. Hastings in 3B. He slouched back to the van, his hands shoved carelessly into the long side pockets of the blue coveralls. He opened the passenger side door and removed a heavy tool box.

"If they asked, we're answering a call to Three-B, name of Hastings."

"Right you are."

"You wouldn't lose your nerve on me, would you, Mr. Babcock?"

The man's round face split in a grin. "Laddie, for three hundred pounds I got nerves of steel."

Back in the building, Carter raced up the five flights and knocked on the door of 5B. Through the hall windows he could see St. James's Park, even make out the ducks on the water.

From the other side of the door he could hear a woman's heels clicking on a hardwood floor, and then the door burst open.

She was tall, thirtyish, with a good face, dark hair, and deep blue eyes. She wore a tailored beige dress and sensible walking shoes. On the floor of the hall behind her were four suitcases.

"Caroline Minor?"

"Yes, but I didn't order service . . ."

"I've got your package from Christobel's," Carter said, and stepped inside, kicking the door closed behind him.

"Who are you?"

"My name is Nick Carter. Cory is in Paris, Caroline; he couldn't risk coming to London. You can trust me."

"Can I?"

"You have to. Do you know you're being watched?"

"Yes, I spotted them this morning. Come in."

Carter followed her past the four packed bags into a room bright with color. "Why the bags?"

"My holiday starts in the morning. I'm visiting my aunt in Scotland."

"Now?"

Her face fell. "I was told this morning that my holiday had been changed. It started today."

"And were you told to go to Scotland?"

"No, but we have to let our superiors know where we

are all the time. It's company policy. How is Cory?"

Just from the way she said it, Carter guessed she had more than a helping-hand interest in Howard. The boy was a charmer.

"Alive. Both of us are, for now."

"Penny Collins and Margery Driver have also had their holidays changed. The three of us are the only ones left at MI6 who worked for Cory."

"Figures. Are they in this, too?"

"No, Cory only asked me for help."

Carter thought for a minute and then said, "Get on the phone and call your hairdresser. Set up an appointment for the day after you return."

"My hairdresser?"

"Do it!"

She grabbed the phone and started to dial. Carter moved to the window and delicately parted one corner of the drape until he had an unobstructed view of the Jaguar.

He paid no attention to the woman's words. When he heard her hang up he parted the drape a little more. Seconds later, one of the men leaned forward and took a hand microphone from the dash. The man spoke, listened, nodded, spoke again, and hung the mike back on the dash.

"What is it?"

Carter turned, moving from the window. "Your phone's tapped. Sit down, Caroline, and let's get to work."

Her grave, handsome face was expressionless as she hefted a briefcase from the floor and set it on a table between them. Silently, she removed reams of computer printouts and carefully laid them out.

"Oh, God," Carter moaned, "I don't think a service call will take that long."

"Don't worry, I have most of the pertinent material in my head. God, I hope Cory appreciates all this. I had a hellish time smuggling all this out."

With a restless swing of her dark hair she started verbally leading Carter through the maze.

At the end of a half hour he went down to the van, supposedly to get a replacement part.

"Which one of these is big and bulky enough to be seen by the Jag?"

"Picture tube, there," Babcock gestured.

Carter grabbed it. "They ask you?"

He nodded. "Major repair, Hastings in Three-B. They seemed satisfied."

"Good show, Mr. Babcock," Carter said with a grin.

Carrying the new picture tube, he returned to the flat.

"Okay, let's finish it off," he said, taking his chair again.

"That's about it, really. The information from 'Klondike' has been invaluable to both MI6 and your CIA."

"And Klondike has never been paid a dime?"

"No, and his identity is known only to Sir Phillip Avery."

Carter picked up one thick sheaf of printout. "But this rundown on Sir Charles's corporate acquisitions matches perfectly with MI6 incoming intelligence on economic conditions, precious metal finds, and so forth."

"Yes, it's obvious Sir Charles had inside information."

"Proof enough," Carter said. "But faced with it, Sir Charles could claim two dozen sources other than Sir Phillip for his source. What about Wolf Longbone?"

"His having access is highly irregular, of course, but not enough to bring more than a reprimand. However, when I cross-referenced everything he had access to or had his name on, I came across a strange thing."

"Yes?"

"The complete personal and research development file

on a man named Anthony Hobbs-Nelson is gone. Even his security clearance and that of his wife, Nanette, has disappeared from Records. It is as though neither of them ever existed. I only discovered it when I came across one of the old sign-out sheets."

"Wolf Longbone signed it out?"

"Yes. I did some checking through Scotland Yard. Shortly after Hobbs-Nelson resigned from MI6, he and his wife were killed in an auto accident. Their Land-Rover went off a cliff in Wales. They were both drowned."

"Any sign of foul play?"

"Not according to Scotland Yard. But it does seem odd, doesn't it, that everything about the man should disappear from Records?"

"It sure as hell does," Carter said, nodding. "What did Hobbs-Nelson do?"

"He played games."

"I beg your pardon?"

"In a think tank," Caroline explained. "Your people have a whole crowd doing exactly the same thing in Washington. You know, 'what if' games. What if there were a famine here or there? What if all the oil in the world were controlled by one company? What if there were a crop failure in the Soviet Union? What if . . . ?"

"Okay, okay, I've got it. Just what kind of games was Hobbs-Nelson playing?"

"That's just it, I don't know. Everything he had or was working on is gone from Records."

"Shit," Carter hissed. "Sorry."

"My sentiments exactly," she said, laughing for the first time since Carter had entered the flat. The movement made a lacy shoulder strap slip from under her dress. She pushed it out of sight with a blush.

Carter kept staring at where the strap had been on her

white skin, a long-ago memory tickling his brain.

First you see it and then you don't.

An afternoon in the War Room at the Pentagon. War games, the results flashing across computer screens and disappearing.

"Caroline, when our people play these games, no matter the outcome, it's automatically transferred in all stages to a computer storage depot in Langley. Do you have the same process?"

Her face was vacant for a moment, and suddenly she shuffled through the printouts and selected one. She flipped through it until she found a number and color-coded index. She studied it and looked up with a broad smile on her face.

"Portsmouth."

"Do their coding readouts correspond to yours in Records?"

"Yes."

"So you could dig out Hobbs-Nelson's stuff no matter how deep it's been buried?"

"I could, but I couldn't get inside the Portsmouth complex without the very highest authority."

"I'll get that. In the meantime, how do you get to Scotland in the morning?"

"BritRail, the ten o'clock train from Paddington."

"Okay, here's what I want you to do . . ."

For the next fifteen minutes, Caroline Minor listened and nodded avidly. By the time Carter left her apartment, she was glowing with the excitement of being a real spy at last.

"How did it go, laddie?"

"One hundred percent, Mr. Babcock. How would you like to make a few hundred more pounds?"

"Telly repair is slow this time of year. Answer your question?"

"I'll need a motorcycle tonight, something fast and powerful, like a BMW."

"My nephew has one. Go on!"

"Can you get a sign painter?"

"My brother. Go on!"

"Can you and your brother make this van look like one of those BritRail catering vans that service the trains?"

Suddenly the old man broke into gales of laughter. "Don't need to do that, laddie."

"Why not?"

"My brother-in-law is a dispatcher at Waterloo Station. We'll ask him for a little loan!"

THIRTEEN

Carter paid off the cab just a few blocks from the Thames and walked through the decaying sprawl of Southwark. After two wrong turns he finally found Dolbien Street and number 12.

The garage was in the rear, more a lean-to shanty than a solid building. But inside everything was as Babcock said it would be.

The BMW was a big, black 1000cc beast with the key in the ignition. Laid out carefully across the tank and seat was a set of men's leathers, boots, and a visored helmet. He found another set, slightly smaller, in the saddlebags.

Babcock and family were earning their money.

Carter stripped, stored his clothes in the empty saddlebag, and put on the leathers. He wheeled the machine from the garage and pushed it about a block before firing it up.

Minutes later he was on Lambeth Road and heading south. On the edge of the city he picked up the M11 and wound the BMW up to 110 miles per hour. It was a dry, star-filled night with little traffic other than slow-moving trucks.

It seemed that no time at all had passed when he

150

zoomed through Harlow and crossed the M25 near Epping. At Redbridge, where the M11 ended, he stopped for coffee.

What he was doing was far from kosher. The instructions were specific: contact no one, wing it, report only to Sir Phillip Avery or John Hutchins.

Well, instructions be damned. They went out the window with Sharon Purdue.

Carter had worked closely with Jonathan Hart-Davis of MI6 many times in the past. Theirs had been not only a good working relationship, but the Killmaster also knew that he had the old intelligence warhorse's friendship and trust. If anyone could open doors and work a miracle or two, it was Jonathan Hart-Davis.

And, Carter hoped, he would do it without asking too many questions.

This was the reason for Carter's late-night ride to Hart-Davis's country place outside Epsom. Because the Killmaster wanted no one to know of the meeting, he had not called MI6 in London first. He had just assumed—because it was Saturday, a weekend—that the man, like all Londoners of his class, would be in the country.

Outside of Redbridge he caught the A24. Now it was a straight shot south on an excellent, lightly traveled road. Carter had the impulse to push the big machine to its 150mph top, but held it in check. With half the police in the world on the lookout for him, it was no time to be arrested for speeding.

Just outside the village of Epsom he had to stop and study a map. He had been to Hart-Davis's country place once, years before, but the maze of tiny, hedgerow-sided lanes in the area could lose a local if he weren't careful.

At last he found what he hoped was the right lane and he was off again. He passed open fields cultivated like children's blocks, farms with the moving shapes of cattle and horses.

Then, about 2 hundred yards ahead, he spotted the two stone pillars that marked the drive he remembered. A shingle on one of the pillars pointed the way.

Carter cut the engine and rolled between them. When he had glided as far as he could, he jumped off and pushed. Near the house he pushed the BMW into the heavy shadows of some trees and checked his position.

It was a million-to-one chance that they would have Hart-Davis staked out, but by this time Carter knew he could count on nothing.

Everything looked normal. The house was three stories, a farmhouse made over into mock Tudor. There were lights burning on the first and second floors.

He emerged from the trees and walked up the wide avenue toward the house. There were two bells. Carter rang them both. The maid or housekeeper who answered was narrow-eyed and opened the door only a few inches. Alarm flashed through her eyes when she saw the ominous figure in black leather.

"Yes, what is it?"

"I'd like to see Mr. Hart-Davis," Carter said. Past the woman, the hall was dark. A suit of armor and helmet stood improbable sentry at the foot of a staircase.

"At this hour?"

"It's very important. I've just ridden down from London."

Suddenly a tall, lean man with distinguished gray at his temples appeared behind the woman. "What is it, Louise . . ."

Carter sighed with relief. "Jonathan, it's me."

The door was pushed open so that what light there was fell across Carter's face. "Nick, what in God's name . . ."

Carter slipped inside, his eyes moving from the man to the woman with caution. The MI6 man caught Carter's meaning.

"It's all right, Louise."

The woman looked oddly at Carter but scurried away. Both men watched her go, and then Hart-Davis turned to the AXE agent.

"Now, what the hell are you doing down here?"

"It's a long story. But first, can your housekeeper be trusted? I don't want *anyone* to know I'm down here, let alone in England."

"Lord, yes, man, she's been with me for twenty years."

"Your family?"

"They didn't come down this weekend."

Carter sagged against the wall. "Jonathan, as we so crudely say in the States, I'm in deep shit."

The other man chuckled. "Not surprising, for you. Suppose we chat over a brandy?"

The long hall curved left and right. Square in its center, a large framed picture of the Queen hung on the wall. Carter followed Hart-Davis through an open door. It was a man's study, with heavy leather furniture, a battered desk littered with papers, pipes and tobacco tins, and an open bar.

Carter fell gratefully into one of the comfortable chairs and Hart-Davis moved to the bar.

There was a small, cheery fire in the fireplace that lifted Carter's spirits. Over the mantel were faded pictures of husky young men with bony knees. In the front row of each, a younger version of Hart-Davis crouched with a rugby football.

Hart-Davis returned with the drinks, passed one to Carter, and took the opposite chair. "Well," he said slowly. "you wanted to see me. I'm listening."

• • •

It was an hour later. They had finished a second brandy and Carter had just about wrapped it up. When he fell silent at last, Jonathan Hart-Davis released a long breath as if it were the only one he had taken in the last hour.

"Anyone but you, Nick, and I would call this whole thing preposterous."

Carter nodded with a wan smile. "I know. But now I'm sure Cory Howard is telling the truth, and I'm sure Caroline Minor's findings point directly to collusion."

"I've known Sir Charles Martin for twenty-five, thirty years. It's hard for me to rationalize that he's behind the whole thing."

Carter shrugged. "There is a possibility that he isn't. It could be that Avery and Hutchins are just using him. That's why I need the Hobbs-Nelson material from Portsmouth. Will you help?"

It was an agonizing two minutes before the MI6 man rose and walked to his desk. He took a pen and wrote for another two minutes. Then he made a quick series of phone calls. Then, taking a ring of keys and a map, he returned to the chair opposite Carter.

"Here is written authorization for this Minor woman to get into the complex. Once inside, the call I just made will give her access to records with her own personal code. You know, of course, that if they have anyone down there in security, they'll be all over you."

Carter nodded. "That's why I need a place close by."

Hart-Davis spread a map of the south coast out on the table between them. "The Records complex is here, at Southsea. My wife owns a little cottage on a small lake, here, near Stoke. It's off the beaten path, and there are no other houses for miles. Here are the keys. Take the map as well."

"Thank you, Jonathan. And Harold Jansen?"

"I just reached him at Oxford. He'll meet you at the cottage at noon tomorrow with his equipment."

Carter flopped back in his chair. "Great. And there are a few things you can find out for me when you get into your office Monday morning."

Using a white, red-tipped cane, Carter tap-tapped his way down the platform at Paddington Station. The mustache, dark raincoat, smoked glasses, and wide-brimmed hat had been the best he could do on short notice, but any disguise was better than none. There was no safe way he could contact Caroline Minor, so the only way to make sure she got safely on the train was an eyeball contact.

He found a partially vacant bench across from the train's only "A" sleeping car, and sat. In his hand a Stratford ticket could be seen by anyone passing.

It was nine-thirty. Beyond the gates for the northbound train, a long line was forming, mostly family groups with bawling children. And then, out of the mass, he saw Caroline.

She was striding down the ramp with her head up, checking her ticket against the numbers on the sides of the coaches. She wore a blue and white dress, a navy cardigan, and carried a single bag.

As she passed Carter, her eyes moved in brief recognition, but her head never turned. A lady going on holiday without a care in the world, Carter thought. Good girl.

He eyeballed her into the coach and watched her through the windows into her compartment. She had barely disappeared when Carter spotted the tail. He was a stocky little guy with a bull neck and wise, cynical eyes. He entered the coach and took a tour through, noting that Caroline was in her compartment. At the other end he stepped off and spoke to a tall, thin one in a trench coat.

Carter held his breath until the thin one nodded and moved away.

There would be only one of them staying on the train. The stocky one got back on and took a seat in the second class coach ahead.

Carter rose and tapped his way to the very last coach on the train, boarded, and took a seat.

Moments later the train jolted ahead. For the next fifteen minutes it rocked west through London. At the Ealing Broadway station, Carter waited until everyone had boarded and the doors were about to be closed before he stepped off.

Still using the cane and adopting a faltering step, he made his way down the steps and through the parking area.

Babcock was parked on the street with the motor running. Carter dived in and the white van lurched ahead instantly.

They had scarcely hit the highway north before Carter was in the back, pulling off the raincoat and dark trousers. Beneath them he wore a pair of white pants and a white, smocklike shirt with the green insignia of BritRail on the left breast pocket.

Back in the front passenger seat, he lit a cigarette. "Good show, Mr. Babcock."

"I'd say that, laddie," the old man chuckled.

"How's our time?"

"We should hit the Stratford station about five minutes before the lady."

They were waiting on the loading dock, the rear of the van facing the train as it pulled in. Through the small panes in the van's rear doors, Carter could see Caroline Minor sitting at a table directly by the kitchen door of the dining car.

The sight brought a smile to his lips. The timing would be perfect. About five minutes outside Stratford they would clear the first class passengers out of the dining car and open it to the rest of the train for lunch.

Hopefully, when the stocky man entered the car he would assume that he had missed Caroline in the passageway returning to her compartment. Even if he didn't make that assumption, it would be another hour or so before another stop was made and he could check her compartment from the outside.

"Here we go, laddie!" Babcock said.

Carter threw the doors wide as the train ground to a halt. Babcock was already out of the van, pounding on the train's matching door and sliding the walkway out.

A gigantic man with a florid face dressed in cook's whites stood in the opening.

" 'Ere, what's this?"

"Off-load, bread and ice cream," Babcock said, mounting the walkway and waving a piece of paper in the man's face.

"What ya say? We're not due 'til Birmingham."

"Change," Babcock barked, maneuvering the cook so that his back was to the dining car. At the same time, he was blocking the view of the salad chef with his own body.

Carter was already scooting past them all with a tray of bread on his shoulder.

"What change, mate?" the chef insisted. "We got too much as it is!"

Babcock shrugged. "Order out of the bakery, I s'pose, too much. Gotta put the bleedin' stuff somewhere."

The argument continued as Carter returned for another tray. Short-and-Stocky was on the platform, smoking. He was turned away from the train. It was obvious that all he was concerned with was the people getting off to check the Bard on his home turf.

Fourth tray set. Out of the corner of his eye he saw a flash of color as the dining car door opened and quickly closed. Caroline darted between the tall bakery trays.

"Next time," Carter hissed. "Ice cream!"

She nodded.

Coming out of the van, Carter tripped. Ten one-gallon containers of ice cream spewed across the kitchen floor.

The cook and salad chef went bananas.

Babcock apologized profusely and Carter tapped Caroline on the shoulder. "Go!"

She did, into the rear of the van like a streaking hummingbird.

Carter came up behind Babcock, slapping him on the shoulder. "Better get on with it, mate. We got two more pickups, ya know."

"Righto, lad. Sorry about the mess, boys!"

While the cook screamed at his subordinate to "Get this bloody mess cleaned up!" Babcock hit the starter. Carter slammed the doors and the van pulled away.

Short-and-Stocky was just tossing away his cigarette and pulling himself up into his coach. He never once looked their way.

"How'd we do, laddie?"

"Like a Swiss watch. You should have been an actor, Mr. Babcock. How long?"

"There's a pullout up here, runs down by the river. About fifteen minutes."

"Good enough," Carter replied, and turned to Caroline Minor. "How . . . ?"

He didn't have to ask. The lady had already pulled the tarp off the BMW and emptied the saddlebags. At the moment, she was in lacy bra and panties, pulling on the leathers.

"Scared?" Carter asked, changing his question.

"Lor', no, I've never had so much bloody fun!" came the laughing reply.

FOURTEEN

It was just after dusk when Carter roared off the A3023 at Stoke and barreled down a tiny lane. It was a narrow secondary road, black macadam, patched and hump-backed. Beside it were hilly fields and gnarled, brown-leafed trees.

"Where are we going?" Caroline asked from her perch behind him.

"It's called Laura's Pond," Carter called back over his shoulder. "Belongs to the wife of a friend."

He had memorized the map, and now he spotted a narrow, rutted dirt lane. A mailbox beside it said Laura's Pond.

He turned in. A mile up the road they crested a hill and dipped down into a clearing carpeted with pine needles.

Carter glided to the side of the cottage and parked the BMW in a gardening shed.

Together they walked around to the front door.

"Isolated enough?" Caroline commented drily.

"That's the idea," Carter said, unlocking the door.

Inside, it was dark, dank and musty. Caroline immediately went around opening windows, while Carter checked the kitchen. By the time he returned to the living room, a sweet breeze was wafting through the windows.

"It's lovely, just like a honeymoon cottage," she said with a grin.

Carter ignored that remark and opened the doors to the bedrooms. "This one's yours. The lady of the house is about your size, if you want to change. Also, you'll need something of hers to enter the complex tomorrow."

Caroline bathed while Carter whipped up a meal. They ate, and then took their coffee down to the edge of the pond about fifty yards from the cottage.

He sat with his back to a tree. She dropped down in the pine needles beside him, a pair of black slacks taut over her rounded hips.

Immediately, Carter launched into a detailed, moment-by-moment recitation of the next morning's exercise. When he was through he went over it all again.

"Got it?"

"Of course. Really, I'm quite bright."

He grinned. "I know you are."

"Pretty, isn't it?" She threw a small stone into the pond, making circular, ever-widening ripples in the still water. "Don't you think?"

"Yeah."

"Not very romantic, are you."

"Too busy being worried."

"About what to do with what we find tomorrow if it's what I think we'll find?"

"That's tomorrow."

Suddenly her hands reached out and drew Carter's head toward hers. She kissed him. Her lips were soft and fragrant and clinging.

When he felt himself sinking, he broke it and stood. "It's going to be a long day tomorrow."

Caroline sighed and fell in step behind him. "Looks like it's going to be a long night tonight."

In the house she moved away to her bedroom.

"Good night."

"Good night."

Carter found the phone and direct-dialed the Paris number given him by Cory Howard. He was twenty minutes ahead of the designated time, but Howard was there and picked up.

"It's me. How're we doin'?"

"I've found him. He's staying in a fleabag over in Montmartre, the Verdun. And guess why?"

"Haven't the foggiest," Carter replied.

"They tried for him, blew his pretty new Citroen all to hell."

"And he lived through it?"

"He wasn't in it. His girl friend was taking the car out of the garage to meet him in front of his flat. The girl friend ended up all over the garage and Liard went underground. I had one hell of a time finding him."

"If he thinks it's his playmates, he might talk easier to you."

"I'm hoping so. I'm going in tonight."

"Watch your back, Cory," Carter growled. "They want everyone out of the picture. They'll be looking for him as well."

"Don't worry about that. Where are you?"

Carter gave him an update and the number of the cottage.

"Let you know how I fare this fine night."

"You do that," Carter said.

"By the way," Howard added, "anything more on our little lass, Sharon Purdue?"

"Got a man working on it first thing in the morning."

"Got a feeling, Nick, she's in up to her pretty head. Later."

"Soon," Carter replied, and hung up.

"Was that Cory?"

Carter turned. She was in the doorway. He was sure Laura Hart-Davis's white peignoir and negligee never looked so good on Laura Hart-Davis.

"Yeah. He thinks he's on to Henri Liard. Between what he can get from Liard and what you get in the morning, we should nail it."

"If your computer man can make sense of it."

"Harold Jansen is the best in the business."

"Mind if I use the phone? My aunt in Scotland is going to be worried sick."

"Sure."

Carter moved past her into his bedroom. He peeled to the skin and lay on the bed in the dark without turning down the covers. He lay there for several minutes, but sleep wouldn't come.

He heard the low murmur of her conversation through the closed bedroom door, and then the receiver hit the cradle.

He waited to hear her door close. It didn't. Instead, his opened softly.

She stood in the doorway. The peignoir floated from her hand. The moonlight was directly behind her, shining through the negligee.

"I don't believe you've got a damned thing on under that," he groaned.

"I don't." A rustling sound and the negligee joined the dropped peignoir.

"Persistent, aren't you," he said.

"Is that what you call it?" She moved to the foot of the bed, then stopped.

"C'mere, dammit."

She floated to the bed and then down to his side. She wound her arms around his neck and drew him close. The eagerness of her lips and fingers lit a blaze inside him. She moved one silky-smooth leg close to his, and the familiar ache began throbbing in his groin.

"How long have you thought about this?" he asked, closing one hand over her breast.

"Since you came to my flat. You didn't think I was going to let something like this pass without getting it all, did you, after months in stuffy Records?"

"Like I told you, it's going to be a long day tomorrow."

In reply, she laughed and rolled upward to straddle his body.

"I don't give a bloody damn, as long as you make it a long night tonight."

In the heat of sexual battle Carter thought he heard a sound outside the cottage. But the powerful desire steaming from her body drove the thought from his mind.

A heavy mist had rolled all the way up to the hills of Montmartre from the Seine. A block from the Hotel Verdun Cory Howard stood in the shadows of a doorway, a cigarette in his lips, its glow dimmed by a cupped hand.

He had been there for a half hour, and for the half hour before that he had stood in the alley behind the hotel. Both spots looked clear.

He had gotten Liard's room number with a phone call during the shift of desk clerks, a lot of gobbledygook about one room number and then another and then the name that Liard was using, Dupré.

It was a corner room, fourth floor. The lights had gone out about twenty minutes earlier.

At last Howard buttoned the flap of his trench coat up to his neck and walked slowly down the narrow street. At the alley he darted in and picked up his pace. A fire escape ran up the side of the hotel. At the first-floor platform he discovered what he had already guessed.

The place was a firetrap. The windows were so painted shut, they were impossible to open.

He moved on up to the top floor and used the iron ladder bolted to the side of the building to reach the roof.

Above the street there was a heavy breeze that blew yellowed newspaper and other light debris from one end to the other. As much by feel as by sight, he moved away from the stone parapet guarding the flat roof. To his right, about dead center in the roof, was a chimney stack. Just on the other side of it he found the trap leading down.

A short flight of wooden stairs took him to a storage room. Several aprons hung by the door, as well as a white cupboard. He pulled the handle. The doors were locked.

He put a knee against the wall and heaved. The doors swung open. The tongue of the lock was still out, but rendered useless by a forgotten bolt. Passkeys, one for each floor and a master linen room key, hung on nails inside.

Howard took the key for the fourth floor and one of the masters. The latter opened the door to the room he was in.

The hall was empty and barely lit by a low-watt bulb. He used the stairs, avoiding the center treads that creaked, and moved down to the fourth floor. Using the butt of his Walther, he popped the bulb, putting the corridor into inky darkness.

At Liard's door he crouched and listened. From the other side came a wheezing sound, interrupted now and then by a cough. Howard couldn't be sure, but the sounds were very much like a knocked-out drunk gasping for air in his sleep.

Cautiously, he inserted and turned the key. He lay on his belly and opened the door only far enough to see into the room.

Henri Liard lay on his back in the middle of a messy bed. He was fully clothed. Beside the bed on the floor were two brandy bottles, one empty, the other nearly so.

Howard slithered into the room, closing the door softly behind him. As he wriggled across the floor, he took a pair of handcuffs from his pocket and pulled his tie free.

Liard was sprawled like an *X*. In seconds one wrist was handcuffed to one side of the bed and his other wrist was tied to the headboard. When this was done, Howard poured the contents of a water pitcher into the man's face and sat on the foot rail.

He came out of it slowly, sputtering, until he saw the figure on the bed.

"No! Oh, dear God, no! Why?...I have done everything you asked..."

"Calm down, Henri." Howard lit a cigarette, holding the flame long enough so the other man could see his face.

Liard stopped struggling to free himself, and gasped, "Howard, you—"

"Did you think I was dead by now, Henri? No matter. If I can find you, they can. It's only a matter of time."

"What do you want?"

"Information. Lots."

"No! *Mon Dieu!* They'll kill me!"

"You damned fool, they'll kill you anyway. They already tried once."

Suddenly Henri Liard could take no more. The good life he had envisioned from his treachery had become a nightmare. His whole body trembled, and then he began to whimper. Seconds later he was weeping openly.

Howard was unmoved. He sat, quietly smoking his cigarette, until it was a butt that he dropped to the floor and ground out with his foot.

"I can get you out of here, Henri, and probably to Portugal or South America. I'm sure you've got funds stashed to live on once you get there."

The crying tapered off. "You'd do that?"

"Yeah. But I won't do it for nothing."

Liard's eyes opened wide and his mood shifted. "What do you want to know?"

"Everything. You fingered us, didn't you?"

A hard swallow. "Yes."

"Who?"

"I don't know, I swear it. I only spoke to them on the telephone. It was always a man or a woman."

"Accents?"

"British. The call was always to an exchange in London, a dead number routed through. The man's voice was low, raspy, very hard to understand."

Wolf Longbone, Howard thought. "And the woman?"

Liard shrugged. "A woman's voice, British. What else?"

"How were you recruited?"

"A telephone call, years ago, right after I went with StarFire. It was the same woman. We met in a Geneva hotel room. I walked in, there was a lamp in my face, she was in the darkness. I never saw her, but it was the same woman. I recognized the voice."

"Good, Henri. Now, besides fingering me and getting Longchamp blown to hell, what else have you done for them?"

Howard lit another cigarette and managed to keep his face calm as it poured out of Liard.

It was hard.

Liard had been privy to almost all of StarFire's dealings: new mineral finds, potential lease purchases, dirt on foreign leaders in Third-World countries they wanted to penetrate, even industrial espionage StarFire had gleaned from their competitors.

All of this had been passed on to London.

My, my, Howard thought. *If they had a man like Liard in every major mining and precious metal refinery conglomerate in the world, they could bring the world to its industrial knees!*

He ground out the second butt. "Why do you think they

decided to dump you, Henri?"

The man's face paled even more and the twitching in his face and body returned. "You'll help me get away?"

"I will."

"StarFire was taken over by a Geneva company, Holderstraf. I went into the computers and started digging. I traced ownership back and found other companies they have taken over."

"Like they did StarFire?" Howard asked.

Liard nodded. "For some time, we've had a key man in Geneva. He works for the government, in the registration office for foreign corporations."

"He could trace the lineage between companies?"

"Yes. I have it all, in my briefcase in the closet."

Howard slid from the bed and got the briefcase, lifting out the contents. It was about eighty pages of computer printout. He only had to peruse a third of it to know that, in the hands of a smart intelligence analyst in international business, the printouts could tell the whole story and probably reveal names.

Howard put the printouts back in the briefcase, locked it, and faced Liard. "They caught you snooping?"

Another long swallow. "Yes."

"You were going to blackmail them for a bigger slice of the pie."

"No. It was only insurance . . ."

"*Merde*, Henri. But no matter, let's get out of here."

As he untied the wrist attached to the headboard, Howard asked casually, "You said you always called London?"

"Yes, always."

"What was the number?"

"Four, four, nine, eight, eleven."

Howard froze, a chill raising the hair on the back of his head.

The number. A contact number. A number he knew so well. Had used so often himself.

In a trance, he moved around the bed toward the hand-cuffed wrist.

He never made it.

There was the single reverberating thud of bone and muscle against wood, and the door shattered inward.

Three of them, two men in front and a woman backup. The men came through first and dropped to their knees. In a split second they had positions, and the high-caliber silenced automatics in their hands started spitting flame.

One man was firing point-blank at a paralyzed Henri Liard on the bed. The second man was leveling at Cory Howard.

They both fired at the same time. Howard felt a burning sensation inside his left leg too near his crotch for comfort. It spun him around and slammed him against the wall, knocking the Walther from his grasp.

His shot had hit home, dead center chest. The shooter's body had fallen backward into the woman's legs, knocking her to the floor.

The second man was jamming a fresh clip into his automatic.

Howard had no time to paw for the Walther. He ran forward and threw himself at the shooter.

His right hand was taut over his left shoulder. Like a snake it moved out, his elbow straightening, the muscles in his forearm contracting.

His target was the promontory of the larynx above the man's Adam's apple.

The blade of his hand struck with a dull thud. It smashed the thyroid cartilage through the wall of the man's throat, killing him instantly.

The body went down with Howard on top of it.

He sensed, and then saw, that the woman had extracted herself from the first shooter and gotten to her feet. Without pausing in his movement, Howard rolled the dead man over him.

Even as the slugs from the woman's gun slammed into the corpse, Howard was painfully pushing his shield toward her.

Then he threw the lifeless, bloody body at her and followed.

She sidestepped the dead missile, but didn't bring the gun up fast enough to stop the live one.

He came up from his crouch, bringing his fingertips together and ramming them swiftly up into her neck. Her feet left the floor with the force of the blow that separated her skull from her spinal cord.

Howard didn't even check. He knew all three of them were dead.

The slug had ripped the hell out of his inside thigh. He would make it if he didn't lose too much blood.

In the bathroom, he stopped the flow with a washcloth and two towels. His trench coat would cover the mess until the towels were saturated and the blood started running down his leg.

Back in the bedroom, one glance told him Henri Liard would never cry again. The shooter had emptied a whole magazine in Liard, starting at his head and ending at his groin.

Howard grabbed the briefcase, found his Walther, and hit the stairs. With his leg, there would be no going up over the roof. He went down, taking the steps three at a time, dragging the leg behind him.

The only real noise had been the shot from his unsilenced Walther. But it was enough. He heard doors popping open and running feet.

The night clerk in the lobby was frantically dialing the phone when Howard hit the bottom step.

Howard put a slug in the wall a foot from his head. The phone went one way, the man the other, out of sight.

The four blocks to his car seemed to take an hour. Thankfully, the streets hadn't come alive with the new day as yet.

He knew a safe doctor in Pigalle, less than a mile away. He would phone from there.

He managed to get the car started and moving. A film was starting to cover his eyes, so the streetlights all came together. Out the driver's side window he took his bearings off the spire of Sacré-Coeur.

It worked. Minutes later he was passing the gaudy neons of Pigalle. Minutes after that he went around the Place de la Chapelle and down St.-Denis. At Rue Cail he turned left and jolted to a stop in front of number 47 with two wheels on the curb.

He looked down. In the illumination of the streetlight through the windshield he could see his lap, all blood down to his knees.

Dragging his leg and clutching the briefcase, he made it up the steps. The bell was answered on the third ring. Dr. Valjean Reschard was used to late-night callers.

"Monsieur le docteur, I hope you remember me . . ."

"Monsieur Howard . . ."

"A telephone . . . I need your—"

It was all he got out. He fainted in the doctor's arms.

FIFTEEN

The building was unobtrusive, sitting in the center of others much like it on Queen Street up against the vastness of Her Majesty's vast Portsmouth naval base. One word was engraved in the stone above the door: MARITIME.

What went on in the four floors above ground had nothing to do with the three floors below ground, where all the vast daily input from foreign intelligence, MI6, was stored.

Carter stood at the bar of a small pub, the Port Sea, across the street. An hour earlier he had let Caroline Minor off at a public restroom in Victoria Park four blocks away.

Inside, she had changed from the black leathers into a green dress and light jacket. The leathers were now in the saddlebags of the BMW parked in front of the pub, and Caroline was in the building.

"Another, sir?"

"Yes, please, and do you have a public phone?"

"In the rear, right beside the men's loo."

"Thanks."

Carter carried his beer to the rear of the pub and fed coins into the phone. The phone rang in Jonathan Hart-Davis's private office only once.

"Central One."

"Hart-Davis, please."

"One moment." She was gone two. "Who's calling, please?"

"Carter."

"Oh, yes, Mr. Carter. There are two messages here for you. One, *Purdue clean, have contacted. Will cooperate. Subject is under constant surveillance.*"

"And the second?"

"Not much, I'm afraid. *In checking other items of our conversation I ran across odd obstacles. Will call back if you call first.*"

"Your boss didn't say what the 'odd obstacles' were, did he?"

"No, sir. He's still down in the Records computer room. Do you have a number?"

Carter gave her the pay phone number. "Tell him to ask for Smiley, but I hope I won't be here very much longer."

He hung up and went back to the bar.

Fifteen minutes later he saw a flash of green at the door, and then she was on the street.

Carter waved the bartender over. "Do me a favor, mate. Name's Smiley. If I get a call on your pay phone, tell my friend that I've gone back to the pond."

"I'll do it."

By the time Carter reached the BMW, Caroline Minor was just turning into Victoria Park. He cranked up and followed.

She was waiting at the loo. Carter pulled up, let the machine idle, and handed her the leathers.

"Nick..."

He followed her stare over his shoulder. Two men in a small sedan had pulled into the street from the side of the maritime buildings. One of them pointed at Carter and the woman and began frantically waving.

"Get on!" Carter hissed.

Caroline drew her skirt to her hips and swung one leg over the seat. The instant Carter felt her arms slide around his middle he released the clutch and the powerful machine lurched forward.

"They're coming after us!" Caroline said when they hit the street. "Fast!"

Carter checked the sideview mirror. The sedan was gaining rapidly.

"That won't last," he growled.

He leaned the machine over until their knees were practically on the ground. Behind him he heard the scream of tires. When he righted, he saw the sedan backing up frantically to make the turn.

It was the last he saw of them. Four turns later he headed back to the harbor and the A3.

Dr. Harold Jansen was definitely a lower-case-type person, the kind who becomes invisible when not speaking. Behind inch-thick glasses he had the washed-out look of an underdeveloped photograph.

But he was a genius.

He had been waiting in the cottage when they arrived, his equipment all set up.

During his tenure at MI6, Anthony Hobbs-Nelson had worked on six "games." Caroline had brought the discs for all six. All but one of the "games" had been completed.

"It has to be this unfinished one," Caroline said.

"Figures," Carter agreed. "Precious metals."

Jansen went to work, with Caroline over his shoulder. Every few minutes she would nervously ask, "Can you finish it?"

The answer was always the same. "I'm sure of it. Computer science has come a long way since this young man devised it."

The phone rang. Caroline dived for it, but Carter beat her to it.

"Yeah, Carter here." In the corner of his eye he saw her move into the bedroom.

"Nick, it's me . . ." Carter could hear the strain in Howard's voice.

"What happened, Cory?"

"They got Liard and put a slug in me. I screwed up, must have led them right to him. But I got the goods, Nick. And that's not all."

"Yeah?"

"Liard's contacts were a man and woman in London. No doubt the man was Longbone . . ."

"We knew that already," Carter said.

"Yeah. But the woman, Nick . . . I recognized the contact number. Nick, it's Caroline, Caroline Minor . . ."

The Killmaster felt the hard muzzle just behind his right ear, and then heard the low whisper. "Turn around, slowly."

He did. She had an earplug in one ear with a tiny antenna sprouting from it. In her left hand was a powerful walkie-talkie. And in her right hand was a Webley .45 automatic. The hand holding it was steady, pointed right at Carter's gut.

"Nick? Nick, are you still there?"

"Yeah, Cory, I'm still here."

"It's Caroline, Nick. She must have just been careless and given me the same contact number to use that she gave Liard and God knows how many others."

"Ask him where he is," she hissed.

Calmly, Carter hung up the phone.

"That's too bad," she sighed, bringing up the walkie. "Wolf, are you there?"

"Yes. We'll have to move at once, just in case. I'm coming in."

"There were two men in a dark sedan following us on the motorcycle."

"I know," said the raspy voice over the walkie. "We intercepted them on the road. They are now in the pond."

The walkie clicked off and Carter's hands balled into fists. He tensed, ready to spring.

"I wouldn't," Caroline said icily. "From this distance I could empty the clip before you get to me."

She was right and the Killmaster knew it. He forced the added adrenaline from his body.

"Miss, just what in God's name is going on?" It was Jansen, still sitting at his computer.

"Shut up, old man, and start breaking down your equipment. You're going to finish the game somewhere else."

"I don't suppose you have an aunt in Scotland," Carter said drily.

"No."

"And you're not on holiday."

"I am on a long leave of absence. So long that I doubt that I'll ever return to musty Records. You were a wonderful coincidence, Carter. Without Cory making his silly extortion demand on Sir Charles, and you being brought in, we might never have gotten the rest of Hobbs-Nelson's little game."

The rear door opened behind Carter. The woman nodded, and powerful hands bent his arms up behind his back.

Then a damp cloth was pressed to his face and he felt his knees turn to water

The room was stark, with paint-peeling walls, dark, high beams, and a rugless floor. Blankets were piled neatly on the foot of the cot where he lay, and there was a small table and two chairs.

All this came to Carter as he slowly came awake.

There were two doors. One was ajar. Through it he

could see a bathroom. Something he desperately needed.

He half walked, half crawled until he reached the bowl.

Nothing came up, no matter how hard he tried. But the pit of his stomach still felt as though it held seven helpings of very hot and very bad Mexican chili.

He turned on the faucet, got it ice cold, and drank and drank from his cupped hands.

That worked. The water came right back up, and along with it the feeling that he was dying. More cold water, this time over his head, and he was able to walk back into the room and check the rest of it out.

There was a tall armoire with drawers. Empty.

He looked up at the single window. It was glass, iron bars, and then shutters. The heavy grillwork made the room as secure as a cell.

He checked the door. It was cut in lateral planks, inches thick and joined on the outside. Short of battering down two or three hundred pounds of solid walnut, there was no way out of the room through the door.

Carter was about to upend the cot and check out the exterior, when a key hit the lock. The door opened and Caroline Minor came in carrying a tray of food. Right behind her was 250 pounds of bull mastiff sporting a machine pistol. Carter guessed that was Wolf Longbone. He was sure when the man spoke.

"Food, wine, eat. It will keep you alive a little longer." The laugh that followed the words sounded like the wheeze of a ruptured bellows.

"Where are we?" Carter asked, holding his seething anger and showing far more calm than he felt.

"Scotland," the woman replied. "Dr. Jansen is coming along quite nicely. By noon tomorrow we should have it all."

"Wonderful, I'm glad for you. Could I have a cigarette?"

"Of course, but you'll have to smoke it while we are in the room."

Carter smiled, accepting the cigarette and pouring some wine. It was all his stomach could handle.

"Just what will you have 'all' of?"

The two of them exchanged looks. The mastiff shrugged. The woman lit a cigarette for herself and took one of the chairs.

"I'm surprised you haven't figured it out for yourself. A few years ago, Anthony Hobbs-Nelson came up with a game to first subvert and then control the governments of ninety percent of the Third-World countries' economies through minerals and precious metals. Oil, gold, uranium are all valuable, but without the precious metals for industry, worldwide business would grind to a halt."

Carter nodded. "I've already figured that much out."

"Wolf was doing research for Hobbs-Nelson. He alerted me to the game. I began lifting his research and prognostications and sending them to my superiors."

Carter's head came up alertly. "Your superiors?"

Her laugh was jarring. "Ah, I see you have realized very little. I have been a rising star in the KGB since I was seventeen years old, Carter, and saw my father die of black lung and my mother scrub the homes that I could never enter."

Carter shook his head. "I've heard all that crap before. What about you, Wolfie? Your old man have black lung?"

The woman answered for him. "No, Wolf is only a product of our Western society. His drive is greed."

The mastiff nodded and showed a gold tooth in a smile.

"My superiors saw potential in Hobbs-Nelson's game, but for obvious reasons it could not be Soviet-implemented."

"So you had Sir Charles Martin implement it."

"Sir Charles was intrigued with the plan. Once again, greed. That same greed had already pushed him into our tent."

Carter poured more wine. "Are you telling me you control Sir Charles's wealth?"

"From the beginning," she admitted with a smug smile. "However, Hobbs-Nelson never got over his anger at MI6 turning down his brainchild. He was going to take the final game to the Americans."

"So Wolfie killed him." The mastiff grinned even more. He had skin like an elephant. "How did Howard and I get into all this?"

"Coincidence, pure coincidence. We had given up any chance of getting our hands on the final two phases of the game, because the variables and Hobbs-Nelson's conclusions were in Portsmouth where we couldn't get at them. We had gone as far as we could go. But then Cory Howard sent his extortion demand and contacted me. It was all made to order if I could get Cory or the agent sent after him to get me into Portsmouth Records."

Carter sat back with a sigh and mashed out the tasteless cigarette. "Which I so conveniently did."

"To my undying gratitude," Caroline said with a smile, standing and moving to the door.

"One big flaw," Carter said. "I've told Jonathan Hart-Davis everything. My guess is he found out something about you. Those two men were chasing you in Portsmouth."

"Perhaps," she said. "But by tomorrow night it will make no difference. I have already sent two coded messages to Sir Phillip Avery and your CIA man, John Hutchins, in your name. Tomorrow night you will meet with them and all three of you will die. Proof will be found that it was Sir Phillip and Hutchins who planned all this to further their careers. You, Carter, will die a hero for uncovering their plot. Hart-Davis may rant all he wants. No one will believe him in the light of what will be found, and it will be his word against a powerful and wealthy patriot, Sir Charles Martin."

Carter poured the last of the wine. "And I suppose you go to Moscow?"

"At last."

She said it with her head high, her lips parted, and an odd, gleaming light in her eyes.

Carter felt sick to his stomach again.

"What about Cory Howard?"

"He's running, but he'll be caught. With you gone, Carter, he has no one left to call." She moved to the door and paused. "By the way, there is no way you could get out of this room. But even if you could, there are two very nasty Dobermans prowling the grounds."

The two of them left and Carter threw up again in the bathroom.

SIXTEEN

Carter ate only because he knew he had to keep his mental and physical strength as close to peak as possible. But it was a strain. Whatever they had knocked him out with had also created a longer term debilitating effect than just sleep.

He surveyed his situation. He was in Scotland and, ten to one, he was probably in a desolate area of Scotland. They had brought Harold Jansen along and were at that moment forcing him to fill in the gaps of Anthony Hobbs-Nelson's deadly economic game.

That was the key.

Once the old man did his job and gave them the final guidelines they needed, the waiting would be over. Carter guessed that Jansen would meet with an "auto accident" to further confuse Jonathan Hart-Davis and the MI6 boys.

It was neat. Too neat.

The fact that the KGB was involved in the mess through Caroline Minor was a monkey wrench the Killmaster had not counted on, had not even taken into consideration. He cursed himself for that, but there was a bit of consolation in the fact that much of what had occurred was, as Minor herself had said, pure coincidence.

But it was coincidence that had worked in the woman's —and her Moscow superiors'—favor.

Now he knew what he had to do. The question was, could he do it . . . and do it in time.

They had emptied his pockets, even taken his shoes. He hadn't so much as a nail file to use as a lever or digging tool. Though, God knew, it would take a jackhammer to dig through concrete and stone a foot thick.

Upending the cot, he crawled atop it to the window. Once there, he opened the two sides of the window inward and reached through the iron grillwork. The latch on the shutters was tricky, but he managed to get it open. The shutters swung wide and he pushed his face against the grill to recon the exterior.

Directly beneath him, a stone portico stood over a courtyard. The courtyard spread left and right, and led to a graveled drive that ended in two huge wrought-iron gates. Spreading each way from the gates as far as he could see was a thick stone wall. Carter guessed it went all around the estate.

If he could get out, how many were in the house besides Caroline Minor and Wolf Longbone? And were there armed guards patrolling inside the walls along with the dogs?

From the slanted beams across the courtyard and the wall, it looked as though every light in the mansion spilled from windows. There were no searchlights outside, but light spilling through those windows from the inside would serve to illuminate any runner.

He checked the casement around the grillwork: wrought iron, embedded deep in the stone enclosure.

Dropping from the cot, he got the fork they had left him to eat with. Back on top of the cot, he scratched at the cement around the bars with the prongs of the fork. It crumbled. The cement was old, very old, and had become brittle.

But, nevertheless, it would take hours with only the fork, and that tool wouldn't last.

Again he checked the door. Not a hinge was visible. All were set on the inside of the jamb. The lock itself had been inset inside the door. There were no screws to work on.

For several seconds he stood in the center of the room, willing his mind to evaluate any possible weakness in his prison.

There was only one.

But how?

Getting through the door, the floor, or the ceiling was a job for a man doing life plus twenty.

The window was his only chance.

Quickly, a plan formulated in his mind. It would make noise, but if it worked, he would be through the window before they could move against him.

He went to work on the cot after pulling the mattress from it. Canvas-covered wooden mattress supports. Quickly, he ripped it off. The sides were sturdy, inch-thick planks, sending his spirits soaring. The ends were mitered and secured with screws.

He tore a strip from his shirttail and wrapped it around the fork until it became a handle. Then he went to work on the screws.

It was a slow, agonizing process, but one by one he got them out. He broke the glue on the corner wedges and extracted the two side planks.

Bound together, they would make one hell of a lever.

Sweating, he tore the blankets into strips. These he used to tightly bind the two side planks together so the stress would always be on both of them together.

Then he set to work on the fork, honing it against the

stone base of the wall. This, too, was slow, but patience and bleeding hands soon paid off.

Finally the handle edge of the fork was sharp enough to cut the canvas into strips. From these he made a sling that went around his butt and his shoulders across the upper, stronger part of his back. When the sling was tied together in front of him, there was still a long tail to tie to the grill.

Then he began to whittle on the ends of the planks, sharpening them. This, too, took an eternity. The wood was stubbornly hard and he had to stop every few minutes to rehone his fork/knife. All of this broken by trips to the door to make sure there were no footsteps in the corridor.

It was the first faint gray light of dawn and his knuckles were bleeding and skinless when he finally had a point he was satisfied with.

He dragged the table over to the window and, standing on top of it, went to work with the sharp end of the fork.

Surprisingly, it was only minutes until he had enough of the cement chipped away so he could get the sharp end of the plank in the crevice.

Using it carefully, he poked, probed, and chipped away until the plank passed easily between the grill and the casement.

Ignoring the pain in his bleeding hands, he strung the canvas tail of the sling through the bars, back and forth, until the pull would be equally distributed.

Despite the need for haste, he took his time choosing a point for leverage with the bound planks. With the noise he would make, he would have time for only two—with luck, three—strong wrenches at the most.

He made a final check.

The planks were in place and they hardly bent from pressure.

Using all the strength in his body, he tested the sling.

The grill actually gave a little from just that amount of pressure.

The fork, now razor sharp, was in his back pocket.

"Okay, genius," he said aloud, "let's see how much physics you remembered."

He took a deep breath and wrenched, twice. He levered with his arms and pulled with all his might until every muscle ached with the strain.

In the quiet dawn, the noise of the grill pulling from the stone was sudden and loud.

He paused, getting his wind and renewing the strength in his aching muscles.

The grill was a third free. It had bit deeply into the planks, but the wood was holding.

He wrenched again, desperately.

Over the clatter as he heaved, he heard running feet outside the door.

The grill sagged, the two horizontal bars its only supports. Jerking out the planks, he battered the grill with the butt.

"C'mon, dammit!"

It worked.

The grill fell to the floor. He cut himself free of the sling and, carrying the planks, hoisted himself to the sill. He crouched there on his heels, framed in the window.

Behind him he heard a key in the door. Below him, the barking of the two Dobermans and running feet accompanied by shouts.

The portico roof was six feet below. Carter dropped lightly, hoping he wouldn't break an ankle.

He didn't, and he was off and running toward the front of the house.

"He's out! There he is!"

The chatter of a machine pistol was simultaneous with

the chipping away at the stone of a chimney just to his left.

Carter ignored it and leaped up to the main roof. Everything now was mass confusion, noise, and chaos below. At the front edge of the main roof, shielded from view of the courtyard, he swung the planks as hard as he could over his head and heaved.

They lit on top of the outer wall, bounced, and went over.

"He's over the wall!"

"Get the gates, bring the dogs!"

Carter crouched down long enough to see two men at the gates. Both had Mauser machine pistols slung to their sides with leather straps. One held the leashes of two huge Dobermans.

From the direction of the window he had just exited he could hear Longbone's raspy voice directing the search.

Toward the center of the roof, he saw a small wooden enclosure and ran for it. There was a wooden hatch inside. He reached for the steel ring and tugged. If there was a bolt or padlock on the other side, he was finished.

It gave.

Pushing the heel of his hand under the hatch cover, he shoved. It moved, noisily, but moved. Only its weight held it down.

In front of the house they still ran around, shouting encouragement to one another. Carter crawled to the blind side of the hatch. He turned on his back and used both hands to heave up the cover. Then he propped it and peered cautiously into the hole. The corridor was a dozen feet below. He could see the carpeting in the dim light from the open door of his own room. He took the weight of the hatch on his shoulder and swung his legs over the hole. For a second he hung by one hand, using head and free arm to prop the cover again. Then he dropped to the floor.

He inched along to the head of the staircase. In front of the open door, lights burned in the hall. Shouts and the noise of running men came from all around the house now. Past the white glare of the hall, the shadows of the passage were a refuge. With luck, all of them would be in the grounds. It was a chance he had to take.

He went down one flight. Nothing. Another. Still nothing.

Then he was on the ground floor in a long, brightly lit hallway loaded with doors. One was open.

Cautiously, he peered in. It was a massive library with a huge stone fireplace. Above the mantel were two shotguns in a rack.

Carter fairly dived for them. Neither was loaded.

"Shit, shit, shit," he hissed, and charged to the end of the room where a behemoth desk squatted in front of a pair of French doors.

One by one, he yanked open the drawers. In the very last one he found a yellow and red box of ammunition.

There were two shells inside. Better than nothing, he decided, and loaded one of the shotguns.

Outside the French doors, a stone porch ran around to another room much like the one he was in. Through the French doors of the other room, Carter saw Harold Jansen sitting at a desk with his equipment before him. He was sweating like a pig and glancing back and forth from his computer screen to a guard who stood over him with a machine pistol.

Carter wanted that machine pistol.

He glided out to the balcony on stocking feet and made his way around.

Just as he was reaching for the knob, Jansen looked up. He saw Carter and his eyes went wide.

The guard saw the change in the old man's face and

whirled, bringing the machine pistol up.

The Killmaster fired the shotgun, both barrels.

Glass, wood fragments, and steel pellets burst into the room, most of the stuff ending up in the guard's body.

Carter was on him in a second. He slung the machine pistol's leather strap over his shoulder and turned to Jansen.

"How many?"

"He's d-dead," the old man stuttered.

"Besides him, dammit!"

"The woman and three others."

"You're sure?"

"Y-y-yes. They've all been in and out of here all night."

"Come on!"

Carter hustled him across the room and shoved him into a closet.

"Stay there, don't move, and don't make a sound."

"You'll come back for me, won't you?"

"God willing and the creek don't rise."

He slammed the door and headed for the one leading to the hall. There were stairs front and back. He headed up.

It was a sure thing the sound of the shotgun would bring them back inside.

He sprinted the length of the house to the front staircase. Just as he hit it, he heard the front door open and then the sound of quietly padding feet on the carpet.

He waited until they were some distance down the hall, and then padded down the stairs himself.

They were moving toward the room he had just left, one on each side of the hall, their backs to him.

"Here!" Carter shouted.

They whirled to face him, making themselves a better target.

Carter sprayed back and forth, cutting both of them practically in half.

The machine pistol clicked on empty. He threw it away and started forward to get one of theirs, when he sensed movement on the stairs to his right.

He dropped to his belly and rolled just as Longbone's rifle fired. The slug hit the carpet inches from Carter's face and he came up with a shoulder in the man's gut.

There was a raspy grunt and the rifle hit the floor. Carter made the mistake of going for the rifle instead of Longbone.

Like a human battering ram, the big man shot his head into Carter's midriff, putting all the strength of his back and legs into the suicidal plunge. Its full force struck with deadly power, and Carter went back against the wall with the crashing and breaking of a table, his head smashing against the wall so hard that his mind went dead and his vision shorted out.

He rolled just in time to avoid the big fist that came out of the air aimed at his face, and gathered his legs to lash out at Longbone's knees. He caught the man too low to cripple him, but felt his feet grate across a kneecap, knowing it would cause pain sufficient to cramp the other man's style for a moment.

Carter remained on the floor. From there he could roll from any blow with more facility than if he were standing up, and oddly, Longbone was more vulnerable than he, if he attacked.

He tightened his muscles for a roll that would allow him to get up before Longbone came to grips with him.

He made the roll, but not quite in time. The big man was in midair, hands out like claws to gouge for Carter's eyes, but he adjusted as he fell, throwing one long leg out to entrap the smaller man. Lightning reflexes, Carter recognized, and he lifted his own foot to catch Longbone's belly or crotch.

There was a numbing weight on his leg, and a painful

wrench at his knee, but Longbone's breath came out in a groaning roar, and he fell like a sack of sand.

Carter was on him in an instant. All in one movement he pulled the honed fork from his back pocket and plunged it through the big man's right eye into the brain.

Caroline Minor.

He saw her in the doorway at the other end of the hall. The Webley in her hand exploded, but the slug went wild. Even a marksman couldn't hit a moving target at that distance.

She disappeared.

Carter ran, picking up a machine pistol on the way. At the end of the hall he heard a roaring engine, and reversed.

Out the front door, he took all six steps in one leap and ran for the gate. He slammed it closed just in time to stop the rush of the two dogs toward him from the woods outside the wall.

Then he turned just as a big Mercedes lurched around the corner from the courtyard.

The twin headlights hit Carter and the machine pistol.

He could barely see her eyes behind the windshield. But he could see enough. She was going through him.

Or she was going to try.

He was thankful that the shattered windshield of the Mercedes obscured his view, so that he never saw the slugs from his machine pistol take off her head.

SEVENTEEN

Greed.

Carter sat in Sir Charles Martin's massive great room listening to it chapter and verse.

Caroline Minor had come to him when she was Sir Phillip Avery's assistant. She had offered him tidbits that would expand his empire. When he was well hooked, she had put him together with Avery in person. Through her, Sir Charles was able to pass selective Soviet secrets that took Avery and, in turn, Hutchins, in.

By then Sir Charles knew about Caroline Minor's Moscow ties. But it was too late. Avery and Hutchins didn't know, but their greed for power in their own agencies made them do whatever Sir Charles asked. And by that time Caroline Minor controlled Sir Charles completely. Even so far as to getting her transferred to Records, where her access to material would be ten times greater.

When the Hobbs-Nelson game came along, it was her chance for the grand coup.

As the broken old man droned on, Carter looked around the room.

A stenographer was taking it all down. Beside her was Jonathan Hart-Davis, his face a mask.

In a chair behind him, Sharon Purdue sat, her eyes vacant. Now and then she glanced up at Carter. But when he would meet her gaze she would look away.

It wasn't really her fault. She just blindly did what she was told. Caroline Minor wanted a progress report on Carter and Howard, and Sharon gave it through Avery, and, in turn, Sir Charles.

Tough, Carter thought. An agent must have logic and common sense, not blind faith.

In a corner, near the bar where he could keep refilling his glass, Cory Howard stood on crutches. Carter could see the hatred in his eyes as he listened to Sir Charles. Now and then he would shift his crutches, but his eyes never left the old man's face.

The Killmaster wondered. Some day, when it had all blown over, when her Majesty's government had quietly transferred Sir Charles Martin's wealth and power to the crown, would Cory Howard come back and exact his revenge on the old man?

Perhaps. But even if he did, it would matter little. He would be killing a corpse.

Carter didn't want to hear any more. He knew how it would all end.

Avery and Hutchins had already been fired. Sharon Purdue had handed in her resignation.

Sir Charles Martin would continue to be a puppet, with another master pulling his strings.

Hobbs-Nelson's deadly little game would be put back in the vault. The Don Quixotes who made up the governments of the West were too humane to bring down a superpower by crippling a lot of little powers.

Quietly, Carter slipped from the room. In an adjoining foyer he found a phone and called the Strand Palace Hotel.

Jova was in her room.

She would be ready in an hour.

Where?

Why, as far as her vast wealth would take them.

That is, until Carter's hands healed and another call came from Washington.

DON'T MISS THE NEXT NEW NICK CARTER SPY THRILLER

TERMS OF VENGEANCE

The lake was shimmering black in the mist beginning three hundred yards before them and ending a quarter of a mile beyond in the jagged rocks at the base of the hill.

"See 'em?" Carter asked.

Sergeant Tom Ebert nodded as he lowered the night glasses from his eyes. "There are two. One is moving along the edge of the lake, there. He does half a perimeter and comes back. The other one's in that thicket, about forty yards back from the lake. I'd say he's working a sound sensor from the way he's been moving."

"They in contact?"

"Yeah," Ebert replied, "every few minutes with walkies. Also, Nick, I'd say there's a third one somewhere as a backup. He probably doesn't show unless they flush something."

Carter smiled and gently patted the top of the cage at his feet. "That's why we have ol' Sly here."

From behind the wire mesh of the cage, the bright eyes of a small red fox stared dolefully out at the two men.

"I'll take the left flank and nail him when he shows himself," Carter said. "You move in as soon as the control man zeroes in on Sly. Give me a count of fifty."

Ebert's darkened face nodded, and Carter moved off silently, being careful to stay outside the effective range of the sound sensor.

Both men wore dull black wet suits with hoods. Their only weapons were West German-manufactured Magnar stun guns, effective up to about twenty-five feet. Tied to the backs of their utility belts were hard-soled oilskin boots, hard rubber cleats attached to the soles. The last piece of equipment was the most necessary: a pair of hard rubber claws that could be attached to the wrist and would extend out over the hands and fingers. The fingers of the claws were long and sharp, and when used properly, acted exactly like the front paws of a cat.

Under his breath, Carter was counting. When he reached fifty he stopped and brought his own night glasses into play.

He barely heard the rustling sound to his rear and right, but through the glasses he saw the control man's head come up alertly. A split second later he brought a walkie up to his mouth.

Beyond the contact man, Carter saw the sentry at the lake take off. With any luck he would spot the fox and drop his guard long enough for Ebert to nail him.

Sound to his left made Carter whirl the glasses in that direction. Ebert had been right. He was just in time to see a sentry in full camouflage gear drop out of a tree and head in the direction given him by the sensor control man.

Carter dropped to his belly and moved forward on a line that would intersect. He did, twenty seconds later, and dropped the man like a tree with the stun gun.

He had scarcely hit the ground before the Killmaster was on him. He strapped the sentry's helmet under his chin and took the battery pack and earphone. As he moved forward, he put the pack in his belt and the plug in his ear.

It was only a receive unit, so he wouldn't have to reply to the control man.

"Kohl, you're heading right for it. Hans, go left . . . no, left, you fool! You're heading right for me!"

Seconds later, Carter was five feet from him, and stood up.

The control man swiveled his head around. "Hans, damn you . . ."

The helmet fooled him for only a few beats, but it was long enough. Before he could unshoulder his machine pistol, Ebert lunged up behind him like a detached shadow and engulfed his face with two big hands.

It took about two breaths and he was out. When the man was limp, Ebert lowered him gently to the ground. He tossed the soaked pad away and placed the man's helmet under his head like a pillow.

"How much did you give him?" Carter whispered.

"Enough for major surgery," Ebert replied, already moving toward the lake with Carter close behind.

They went into the water side by side, and breast-stroked across. A low stone wall ran along the water's edge. They stopped just short of it, and both of them took small, battery-powered pulseometers from under their suits. Carter squinted at the jumping needle and looked up at the top of the wall.

"There . . ."

"And there," Ebert said. "About four feet apart, going two ways."

They walked directly to the wall and raised their hands, poising the small instruments together.

"Ready?" Ebert nodded. "Now!"

As one, they set the pulsers down on top of the wall and anxiously watched as the needles kept up their rhythmic jumping as they intercepted and reflected the silent pulsations from the other two already on the wall.

One at a time they scrambled over. When the boots and claws were in place, they started up. Though the rock face was sheer to the eye, up close there were edges and even holes of erosion caused by centuries of weather. The climbing was much easier than they had expected. It took just less than a half hour to reach the upper wall.

Again, a pulser was used to check for sensors. When none was found, they began to work their way around to the side below the conference room.

"There may be dogs," Ebert hissed.

"I'm sure there are," Carter whispered, "but more than likely they're kept just for sniffing out explosives. When they're not being used, they're probably kept in the courtyard on the other side. Up you go!"

Carter boosted Ebert to his shoulders. The sergeant was able to get a good grasp on the top of the wall. When he did, Carter crawled right up his legs and over his body. When he was flat out on top, he helped Ebert up.

Head to head, they lay on top of the wall. Below them was a small courtyard. On the inner side were steps leading up to the next level, one below their objective.

Silently, they dropped into the courtyard and padded across. Just short of the steps they paused to unscrew the rubber cleats. This done, they tied the claws back to their belts and continued.

An iron gate, padlocked, barred them at the top. It took fifteen seconds for Carter to pick it.

They were in the walkway directly below the conference room. The wall up was made of uneven stone. Between where they stood and the base of the windows was about forty feet and two ledges.

It was the easiest part.

Again, Carter used the pulse detector.

Nothing.

They started up, and just as they hit the first ledge Carter knew it was all over.

There were over a hundred roosting pigeons. Half of them were frightened into flight, and the other half raised a din that could be heard a mile away.

Spotlights came on from both nearby towers, illuminating the entire wall and the two human flies clinging to it.

It wasn't five seconds until the walkway below them was filled with armed men. The windows above them opened and more machine pistols pointed down at them.

"Climb down slowly! Let me warn you, any offensive move and you will be shot!"

"Goddamned pigeons," Carter muttered. "The oldest alarm system in the world."

> —From TERMS OF VENGEANCE
> A New Nick Carter Spy Thriller
> From Jove in September 1987